LOVE AWAITS

A TALE OF UNBROKEN PROMISES

HARSHITA NANDA

Made with ♥ on the Notion Press Platform
www.notionpress.com

Contents

Contents

ॐ

"What is love?" asked the Rose.
"I do not know," said the Nightingale.
"It is a mystery."
The Nightingale and the Rose by Oscar Wilde

ॐ

I

I wish I could remember the first day,
First hour, first moment of your meeting me.

Fluffy white clouds drifted lazily through a brilliant blue sky. The early morning sun spread its benevolent rays from behind peaks covered in verdant forests surrounding the bus stand. A cool breeze blew away the diesel fumes that usually enveloped the inter-city bus stand. Beneath the growling of the engines, one could even hear the warbling of the birds. It was the kind of welcome that most people wanted when they visited this small town nestled in the Himalayas. The tourists tumbling out from the early morning bus from the city were laughing and chattering, their spirits uplifted by the beauty of nature surrounding them.

All except one.

The holiday started smoothly when Mira boarded the late-night bus from the city to the hill station. Waking to the soft morning light, she eagerly watched from the window as the bus drove along the narrow, deodar-lined mountain roads. Her heart lifted on seeing the majestic trees soaring to the sky as she imagined days doing nothing but wandering amongst them. But the insistent ringing of her phone just as the bus pulled into the town's bus stand broke the spell. Her boss had called, demanding she fix a presentation. Mira being on holiday was an inconvenience, but the work couldn't wait, he said.

Thus, the Mira, who got off the bus, was no longer the light-hearted Mira who had boarded the bus eight hours before. This Mira had two lines on her forehead as her sneaker-clad feet tapped on the pavement, waiting for her suitcase to emerge from the boot of the bus.

"Stupid curmudgeon. He knows I am on leave, and even then, he wants me to overhaul a presentation! I swear I will quit this job the moment I return," she muttered.

Her boss's demand–the email had to arrive by noon–echoed in her mind. Making a face, she tied her silky, shoulder-length hair with a scrunchy in a high ponytail. Pushing the sleeves of her green oversized pullover above her elbows, she grasped the handle of her pink suitcase, dragging it across the pavement to reach the entrance of the bus stand.

Ignoring the crowd of taxi drivers and autowallas, promising her good deals on hotels, her eyes scanned the shops of the bazaar abutting the bus stand. They zeroed in on a *Free Wi-Fi* sign painted on a glass window. She peered closely at the faded signboard swinging above. It read Sunshine Coffeehouse. Her stomach chose that moment to let out a grumble, reminding her she had yet to have her morning meal.

Holiday and the cute homestay she had booked would have to wait. She had this pesky email to send. More importantly, she needed breakfast. Ignoring the surrounding chaos, she set course for the cafe.

The bell of the coffeehouse's door tinkled as Mira opened the door. She held the door open with one hand while pulling her suitcase with the other. The door sill snagged the suitcase's wheels. With the scent of coffee in the air tempting her, she refused to quit and heaved on the handle. She almost lost her balance, but finally, she and the suitcase were inside. Tucking the strands of hair that had escaped from her ponytail behind her ear, she massaged her shoulder, which screamed at her for pulling a loaded suitcase over a road that had more potholes than the moon, as her eyes flicked through the cafe. She groaned inwardly to see all the tables were occupied.

Her eyes narrowed on a table in the back, where an elderly gentleman sat alone, reading. There was an air of stillness around him, contrasting with the bustle and chatter around him. Desperate to find a seat, she walked towards him. "Uncle, do you mind if I share the table with you? I urgently need to finish some work, and all the other tables are occupied."

The gentleman looked at his watch and said, "I am waiting for someone, but you can have the seat, *beta ji*."

Giving him a grateful smile, Mira sank into the chair opposite him. She opened her laptop, and the gentleman went back to reading his book. As her fingers flew over the keyboard, she couldn't help but notice that whenever the door opened, the man glanced towards it.

Mailing the presentation, Mira called a server to place an order.

"A cappuccino with a vegetable sandwich, please," she said. "Uncle, may I order something for you? My treat for letting me share the table."

"No, *beta ji*! I need nothing," he replied, shooting her a smile before going back to his book.

Waiting for her coffee, Mira scrolled through her phone, but instead of watching reels, she surreptitiously observed the gentleman in front of her. His wispy white hair and tweed coat reminded her of the character Carl from the movie Up. But while Carl was grumpy and gruff, this man's tone, in the few words he had spoken to Mira, was soft and cultured. There was an aura of old-world courtliness around him that charmed her.

The door tinkled again, and a few tourists walked in.

The gentleman looked up, but once again, it was not whom he was waiting for. A soft sigh escaped his lips as he turned his attention back to the book. If Mira had not been looking at him, she would have missed the imperceptible slump in his shoulders.

Intrigued, Mira leaned forward, placing her elbows on the table. "What time is your friend supposed to come, Uncle?"

Giving a rueful smile, the gentleman said, "At eleven, but since it is already noon, I doubt they will come now."

"Can't you call and find out?" she asked.

"I don't have their number," he replied.

Mira was taken aback. In today's digital age, how was this possible?

"Maybe you can contact a friend or a family member?" she persisted.

He shook his head.

A husky voice interrupted their conversation.

"*Dadu?*"

Mira turned to see a tall, bespectacled man holding a tray near their table. He was wearing a blue button-down, checked shirt tucked into dark trousers. His broad shoulders, straight back and the air of confidence around him told Mira that this man was not a helper at the coffeehouse.

"Manan!" the gentleman said, closing his book. "I guess it is time for me to go home."

Giving a small bow in Mira's direction, he tucked his book under his arm and walked out.

"Your order, ma'am," the man called Manan said, placing the tray with a toasted sandwich and the steaming cup of coffee on the table. A lock of dark hair fell on his forehead, giving a softer edge to the harsh lines of his face.

As he turned to leave, Mira placed a hand on his sleeve to stop him. The old man had piqued her curiosity, and she wanted to know more about him.

"Is Uncle your grandfather? Who was he waiting for? How come he doesn't have their number?" The questions tumbled out of her mouth one after the other.

Manan looked at her hand on his sleeve, his brow arching at her familiarity with a stranger.

Embarrassed, Mira flushed and removed her hand.

Glancing at the suitcase Mira had tucked near her chair, he asked, "Tourist, right? I saw your struggle with the doorsill."

Not expecting an answer from Mira, his lips curled with disdain. "Hope you have a good time sightseeing in our town," he added. The crispness of his tone was in sharp contrast to the earlier warmth of the gentleman.

Dumbfound, Mira stared as Manan walked away. *The sheer gall of the man! He saw my struggle and didn't help! To top it all, the condescension in his tone!* Mira wanted to give him a piece of her mind but decided against it. *Considering how my day is going, I might embarrass myself even more.*

Deciding to skip breakfast, she placed some money on the table. The bell on the door jangled as she slammed it shut on her way out.

II

I have been here before,
But when or how I cannot tell.

The urgent chattering of the magpies outside her window woke Mira. She stretched languidly under the light quilt, looking at the blushing sky from the window she had left open last night despite the cold. Some might say it was too early to wake up when one was on holiday, but Mira didn't mind. She enjoyed such early mornings when she could observe the world waking up with no deadlines niggling at the back of her mind. All she had to look forward to the next few days was to soak in the atmosphere of the hill town she had picked for a holiday.

Picking up an embroidered shawl, she wrapped it snugly around her as she padded to the balcony. The cold air felt invigorating as she settled on a chair, her eyes following the antics of the birds as they flitted, chattered, and gossiped with each other. A few brave ones hopped closer to her, anticipating she would drop a tidbit or a morsel. They eyed her gravely for a few minutes before giving a squawk of disappointment and flying away. Looking at the birds hunting for crumbs made Mira remember the holidays with her parents.

They would wake up early to see the sunrise, enjoying their first cup of tea together. Ma always carried biscuits and homemade goodies on such trips. After tea, she would always drop crumbs of biscuits for the birds. Amused, Papa would laugh, saying she was spoiling the tastebuds of the birds by giving them posh biscuits to eat.

Mira closed her eyes against the pain that stabbed through her heart. It was in moments like these, when she was alone, that she felt their absence keenly. The only daughter of a couple who had eloped to marry, her parents had been her only family. She remembered how excited she was that day before a phone call brought her whole world crashing down.

She had just bagged an offer at her university job fair and was planning to surprise her parents with the news, who were driving down to see her. But they never reached her. A fatal road accident snatched them away from her. At twenty-one, Mira became an orphan with a gaping hole in her heart and life. She spent the last semester of college trying to overcome the trauma and function as an adult when all she wanted was to hug her parents for one last time. After she started working, one thing that helped her overcome her grief was the solo vacations she took every six months, just like when her parents were alive.

She always picked homestays over hotels for these holidays. The families she stayed with were strangers, but it helped her retain her sanity. She knew it was an illusion, but for a few moments at least, she felt as if she was part of a unit.

A knock on the bedroom door brought her back to the present. It was the homestay Aunty calling her for breakfast.

After breakfast, dressed comfortably in a long-sleeved tunic and jeans, Mira set out to explore the town. Mira enjoyed walking through the narrow lanes bordered by hedges and trees, inhaling the crisp air. Still an undiscovered gem, people could walk through its streets without jostling with the hordes that seemed to descend the popular hill stations every long weekend. However, ignoring all the places of interest in the town recommended by Aunty and TripAdvisor, Mira's sneakered feet, out of their own volition, walked towards Sunshine Coffeehouse.

The bell on the door tinkled softly as she pushed it open. With her stomach full and no urgent emails to be sent, she could pay attention to the interiors she had missed noting the previous day.

Black-and-white tiles covered the floor of the square room. The tables, made of highly polished dark wood, contrasted with chairs covered in well-worn chintz cushions. The old-fashioned lamps and exposed electric wires added to the quaintness.

The coffeehouse was half-empty, but the old gentleman was there, reading a book at the same corner table. Mira gave a wary glance around. The other person, Manan, who had been so rude yesterday, was nowhere to be seen.

Good, Mira thought, *I don't want to see his smug face, even though he does look ruggedly handsome in his rimless glasses.*

Mira ruthlessly quashed the traitorous thought before walking over to the gentleman. "Hi, Uncle! Remember me? I shared your table yesterday. Thank you so much for your help! My name is Mira," she said with a bright smile.

The gentleman looked up from the book he was reading. He smiled, "Of course, *beta ji*, I remember. It is polite of you to come and say hello to an old man. My name is Raghunath Sharma, a retired professor of English."

"Oh, how fascinating!" Mira replied, slipping into the chair opposite him.

Mira and Raghunath soon slipped into an easy conversation about books. But ever so often, Raghunath sneaked a look at his watch or the door. At about twelve-thirty, Manan came to their table. Mira looked at him from the corner of her eye, trying to ignore the whiff of his musky cologne that wafted towards her.

Ignoring her, Manan placed a hand on Raghunath's shoulder.

"Manan!" Raghunath's eyes lit up with pleasure. Patting Manan's hand, he continued, "*Beta ji*, Manan owns this coffeehouse."

Manan gave a short nod to Mira before turning to Raghunath. "Time for you to go home, *Dadu*."

Raghunath sighed before nodding his head. "It was great to chat with you, my dear," he said to Mira, before picking up his book and walking out.

Mira's smile at Raghunath's adieu faded as she felt Manan's eyes on her. She glanced up to see that irritating left eyebrow of his cocked up. His expression made Mira feel like a little girl caught with her hand in the cookie jar. Almost as if he was judging her for talking to Raghunath and finding her guilty. Annoyed by the awkward silence between them and the way Manan's cologne made her tongue tie itself up in knots, she muttered a hasty goodbye and left.

Day three was the same as before. After breakfast, Mira set out to explore the town but, once again, found herself in the coffeehouse. Raghunath was reading at his usual corner table. At twelve-thirty, Manan came, and Raghunath bid a courteous goodbye before departing.

Looking at Raghunath shuffle through the crowded tables, Mira felt curiosity tingling through her spine. She didn't know why, but her heart insisted she needed to know why and for whom Raghunath waited every day. But she only had a few more days left in town.

Wondering if she could risk asking again, she looked at Manan. She found him looking at her. His left eyebrow was, once again, raised as he nodded towards the door. There was a line of people waiting for tables. Getting the hint, Mira picked up her bag and walked out. She mentally patted herself on the back when she didn't let Manan's expression aggravate her into slamming the door on the way out.

On the fourth day, after Raghunath left, instead of waiting for Manan's left eyebrow to shoot up, Mira decided to be bold. Turning towards Manan, she said, "Look, I know you don't like me, and I am a stranger in this town. But funnily enough, I like Raghunath Uncle. I know it is too early. I have known him only for a couple of days, but I have started counting Uncle as a dear friend. So, can you please tell me who he is waiting for?"

Manan looked at her without saying a word.

"Please? I have no ulterior motive," she cajoled, giving him a smile that had melted many a crusty heart. "Watching him wait, day after day, without knowing why, is breaking my heart and driving me mad!"

Manan looked at the woman, who had appeared at the coffeehouse a few days before and, for some reason, kept coming every day. He wondered what it was about her that made Raghunath talk to her with so much familiarity. Of average height and ordinary looks, she was not conventionally pretty. But when she laughed and conversed with Raghunath, there was an animation about her that made one want to be close to her.

Taking off his glasses, Manan polished them as he sat on the chair Raghunath had just vacated. "I don't know why you are doing this, but you seem to have made an impression on *Dadu*. You spend time with him and listen to what he says. I have never heard him talk about any of the guests at home. He seems to like you, and I think, thinks of you as a friend."

He paused, his gaze steady on her. Mira felt drawn by his eyes, which resembled fathomless pools of chocolate. She suppressed a disappointed sigh as he placed his glasses back on, hiding them from her.

"So, for his sake," he continued, "I will share his story. *Dadu* is waiting for the love of his life, Janaki.

III

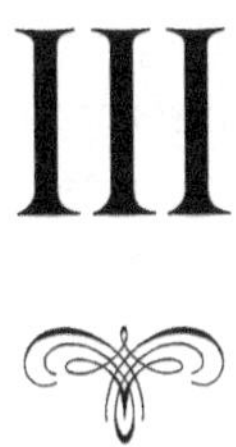

My face in thine eye, thine in mine appears,
And true plain hearts do in the faces rest;

Clutching books and papers with hands that were getting numb in the chilly mountain air, Raghunath walked briskly down the mountain road towards his college. He was already running late, and Professor Acharya was liable to throw a fit if someone walked in late for his class, even if it was his teaching assistant.

Another year, Raghu promised himself. Another year and his PhD would be complete. He would emigrate to the greener pastures of the US, where his knowledge and talent wouldn't be suppressed by the petty politics of a small-town college.

Lost in his thoughts, Raghunath stumbled over the uneven steps at the college gate. Books and papers slipped from his hands, scattering on the ground. Cursing under his breath, he gathered them hastily before running towards the classroom as the college clock boomed out the hour.

Thankfully, he arrived a few minutes before Professor Acharya. He had just finished setting up the projector when the professor walked in. Raghunath nodded to him before going to the back of the classroom.

The professor had just started on the first slide when a voice interrupted from the doorway.

"Excuse me, Sir."

With an annoyed huff, the professor took off his glasses to look at the speaker.

It was a young woman.

"Yes?" the professor asked, his voice gruff.

"Is there a Raghunath Sharma in this class, sir? I found a few papers with his name near the college gate."

Raghunath was amused at the interruption, for interrupting Professor Acharya's class usually meant a tongue-lashing. But when he heard his name spoken, he jumped to his feet, hurrying to the doorway. Barely glancing at the young woman who held out the papers, he grasped them when their fingers brushed. Immediately he felt a jolt of electric current pass through him. Surprised, he looked up to see deep brown eyes staring back at him. Eyes that seemed to mirror the same shock he had felt when their hands had brushed. Oblivious to their surroundings, they stared at each other, bemused.

An irate clearing of the throat brought them back to reality.

"Thank you," mumbled Raghunath. The woman nodded before walking away.

Ignoring Professor Acharya's baleful stare, Raghunath walked back to his seat, his senses humming. He felt disoriented as if his world had tilted from its axis.

The moment the lecture was over, Raghunath rushed out of the classroom, his eyes searching the college grounds to find the young woman. But she had disappeared.

Raghunath spent a restless night tossing and turning. Whenever he closed his eyes, the image of the young woman popped up. He wondered who she was and why he had felt the way he did when their hands had touched. In her simple blue cotton saree and hair tied neatly in two plaits, she was like the other girl students he was used to seeing on the campus. The ones that, until now, he had never paid attention to. But something about her unadorned face, devoid of any bindi or Kajal, made him think about her. It might have been in the sharpness of her nose, the smoothness of her skin which was the colour of milk, or eyes that shone with intelligence.

The next morning, Raghunath reached college earlier than usual. He, once again, searched all over the campus before finally finding her in the library, seated at one of the window alcove tables, engrossed in a book.

Seeing her looking radiant in a lemon-yellow saree, Raghunath felt like the sun had burst from behind the clouds on a gloomy day. Raghunath walked closer, wondering how to approach her, when, in turning pages, she looked up, and their eyes met.

Raghunath felt the same frisson of awareness that he had felt the day before.

He hesitated and then saw a faint colour rising on her cheeks. Taking courage from the blush, he went closer and said, "Thank you for yesterday. I am sorry, I was so surprised that I couldn't even thank you properly. My name is Raghunath, and I am a PhD student under Professor Acharya."

The pink on her cheeks deepened. "I am glad I could help," she replied softly. Hesitating a little, she added, "My name is Janaki. I am in first-year English."

"Would you like to go for a cup of coffee? As thanks for helping me!" Raghunath hastily added lest she misconstrue his motives.

Janaki's eyes refused to meet his, and she took so long to answer that Raghunath figured she would say no, but then, she nodded a slow yes. "I have half an hour before my next class."

They sat opposite each other, slowly sipping their coffee. The silence between them stretched as they glanced at each other furtively. Both could feel a connection but didn't know how to break the silence.

Janaki surreptitiously checked the time on her wristwatch. Conscious of the time running out, Raghunath blurted, "If you need help with any assignment or project, you can ask me."

Desperation made his voice a little too loud, making Janaki widen her eyes.

"I mean, because you helped me. Plus, you are studying English, and that is my field..." Raghunath's voice trailed off, unsure of whether he was coming as friendly or creepy. Janaki did not look very comfortable at his offer of help.

"I just want to help," he added, softly.

Janaki mumbled a "hmmm," picking up her cup to take a sip. Something glinted on her finger. It was a diamond ring.

"That's a pretty ring," he casually remarked, grateful to have found a new topic.

Janaki placed the cup down to stare at the ring. "It is my engagement ring. My wedding is fixed for the eighteenth of next month."

Raghunath couldn't believe his ears. Janaki was getting married! But he had just met her! He wanted to know more about her. He wanted to explore this connection between them.

"Sorry, the coffee was a mistake," said Janaki, understanding Raghunath's shocked expression. "I should have told you I was engaged to be married."

She shifted in her seat as if to get up. Raghunath shook his head, trying to process Janaki's statement.

"Hey! It's OK," he said in a calmer tone. "It is just a coffee to express my thanks. Two individuals can have a cup of coffee together without romantic undercurrents. I am not declaring my undying love for you! Why don't you tell me about your fiancé? And what about your studies? Hope you will finish your education?"

Raghunath's smile hid the turmoil in his heart.

"I don't know much about my fiancé. He is in the army and will come to town two days before the wedding."

"I have a lifetime to know him," she added in a low voice.

Raghunath nodded weakly at her words.

They were quiet as they finished the rest of their coffee before heading their separate ways.

Janaki's approaching marriage couldn't dislodge her from Raghunath's mind. He would search for Janaki whenever he would be on campus, his heart leaping with joy whenever he would catch a glimpse.

Some days, he would feel someone was watching him, turning, he would see Janaki looking at him. Their eyes would hold for a few seconds before Janaki would look away in studied indifference, but a few minutes later, she would again try to sneak a look.

It was almost four weeks since their first coffee together when Janaki stopped coming to college. Raghunath's heart plummeted when he realised her wedding was the reason for her absence.

The days dragged on, gloomy and damp, just like his mood. Every day his eyes would scan the grounds and corridors of the college for her. Hoping, willing Janaki to be back. Not finding her, his heart would plummet. He struggled with the edits of his thesis and his teaching assistant duties.

She had said she would complete her degree from here. So where was she, and how long did it take to get married? He argued mentally with himself. Raghunath knew he was being childish. He didn't even know Janaki properly, but the connection he felt with her was inexplicable. It seemed to permeate his entire being.

One day, after weeks of rain, the sun shone through the clouds.

Raghunath saw her near the entrance of the library, chatting with her friends. His heart leapt with joy as his feet moved quickly towards her before coming to an abrupt halt.

She had changed.

A black beaded necklace adorned her neck, gold bangles tinkled on her wrists, and a red dot shone in the middle of her forehead. She was now married to someone else. Raghunath was just another stranger.

Janaki had noticed Raghunath walking towards her, first with unabashed pleasure and then with growing alarm. Despite how her heart felt at the sight of Raghunath, she knew she needed to suppress these feelings. Steeling her heart, Janaki pointedly turned away.

Taking the hint, Raghunath pivoted and walked away in the opposite direction.

IV

Time continued to fly as Raghunath tried to put Janaki off his mind. He avoided searching for her on campus. And if he saw her, he would look away.

To move on with his life, he even agreed to a match picked by his mother. He knew that whatever unnamed emotion he felt for Janaki, it was not love. If it had been love, then fate would not have been so cruel to put her in his life and then bound her by seven vows to another man.

But despite all his efforts, he couldn't avoid seeing her when one day, Professor Acharya called him into his office. Seated across from the professor was Janaki, her eyes fixed on a spot behind the professor's balding head.

Looking up at his entry, the Professor said, "Ah, yes! Raghunath! This is Janaki. She wants to do a project on medieval literature and feminism. Please help her with the resources and guide her in the project. I know it is not your area of expertise, but her husband asked for the best, and there is no one better in the department."

Raghunath searched for an excuse to give to the Professor. He didn't want to work with Janaki. Judging by how Janaki was avoiding looking at him, he knew Janaki was also finding Professor's suggestion uncomfortable.

"Sir, you asked me to grade the second-year literature mid-semester papers. I don't think I will have the time to help."

"Nonsense! Don't worry, you will manage, I am sure. I will see both of you a month from now with the completed project. Good luck!" Professor Acharya dismissed Raghunath's excuses with a wave of a hand.

Five minutes later, Raghunath and Janaki stood outside the professor's chamber. Janaki pulled the *pallu* of her green saree closer around her, her fingers clenching its edge tight. Her eyes were fixed on the ground in front of her. Looking at the discomfort in her body language, Raghunath ran a hand through his hair. He wanted to walk away. From this unnecessary task. From the college. From Janaki.

Curse this college and its professors who keep piling on work on me without asking whether I want to do it or not! Raghunath thought, turning his back towards Janaki. The silence between them stretched and grew until Janaki's soft words reached his ears.

"I am sorry that Professor Acharya put you on the spot. I had casually expressed a desire to do a project like this to my husband. Without telling me, he approached the Professor who is a family friend. You don't have to help me.

I think I can manage by myself."

"And what if your husband complains to the Professor that I am not helping you?"

"I will not tell him."

Half-turning towards her, Raghunath sneered, "Keeping secrets from hubby dearest already?" He was unable to avoid hurting her with his only weapon. Words.

Janaki's cheeks flamed red, but she stayed silent, her eyes still not meeting his.

"The future of my hard-earned degree is hanging in the balance. I have enough professionalism to do the work assigned. I will point out some books to get you started," Raghunath said, briskly turning towards the library. He did not bother to look back and see if Janaki followed him.

The loud thwack reverberated through the library as Raghunath slapped a stack of books on a table.

Ignoring Janaki's flinch, Raghunath brusquely said, "Read these books and have an outline for the report ready by the end of the week."

Janaki dug into her bag pulling out a folded piece of foolscap. "I tried making a rough outline. If you could glance and let me know if I am on the right track."

Raghunath looked at the paper, tempted to reach out and take it from her. Instead, his lips curled. Tapping the books with his forefinger, he repeated. "Read them and prepare an outline by the end of the week." Unable to stop the curt words as they dropped one after the other, he added, "Let's see if the Professor's special family friend has it in her to do the project. Or not."

Janaki's lips tightened as the barb hit home. Raghunath felt like an ass the way Janaki shrunk into herself at his words. As if he had physically hurt her. Ignoring the discomfort in his heart on seeing the hurt in her eyes,

Raghunath walked out of the library.

He needed to get far away from the annoying fragrance of her lavender perfume that made his blood sing.

****

How could one be so eager and yet dread to meet someone? Raghunath thought, dragging a comb roughly through the mop of his curls. It was Friday, and after a few days of avoiding Janaki, he needed to meet her in the library to discuss the project outline.

The half-hour he had spent earlier in the week in the library showing Janaki the books had been the worst, and yet the most important, half-an-hour of his life. Thirty minutes alone with her, in the space he loved and treasured. He wanted to share its treasures and point out the books he loved, but the black beaded necklace, half-hidden in the *pallu* of her saree, taunted him. The attraction he felt towards her made him uncomfortable. It made his words cruel, disparaging her abilities, and dimming the joy in her eyes.

The only way out of this emotional quagmire, Raghunath realised, was to throw himself at the mercy of Professor Acharya and beg him to excuse Raghunath from helping Janaki. Now that he had given her the books, it wasn't as if Raghunath had left her high and dry.

Raghunath's decision, however, crumbled the moment he walked into the campus and saw Janaki laughing with her friends. She was once again wearing the blue saree she had worn the first time they had met. Her long hair was confined in a low bun at the nape, showing off the elegant lines of her neck. The tinkle of her laughter floated over to pierce Raghunath's heart. His steps slowed before coming to a stop a few feet from her.

Janaki looked up at that moment. Her laughter faded, but a shy smile hovered on her lips as she gave him a small nod of acknowledgement.

It is only for a month. What harm is there in working with her on the project? His heart whispered.

Hearing his heart, Raghunath's feet decided to rebel against his mind. They started moving in Janaki's direction. His lips, too, joined in the rebellion as they curved in reply to Janaki.

*****

"Can you go over the report?" Janaki asked, handing the papers to Raghunath seated across from her in the library.

Janaki and Raghunath had fallen into an unspoken pattern of meeting every day at eleven in the library to work on the project. After a month, the project was done, and Janaki was supposed to submit the final report by the end of the day.

In the past few weeks, as Raghunath discovered different facets of Janaki's personality, his attraction for her deepened. Meeting Janaki for half an hour in the library had become the highlight of his day.

"Is it ok? Should I rewrite the paragraph before the conclusion? I think it is too meandering. Do you think I should add more references?" The words tumbled from Janaki's lips, accompanying the rhythm of the pencil as she tapped it repeatedly against the table.

Raghunath wanted to place his hand on top of hers and give it a squeeze, partly to stop the tapping but also, because he wanted to calm her nerves.

Ignoring his need, he said, "Janaki, you are blabbering!" Tempering his words with a smile, he added, "I know it would not have been easy balancing your domestic duties and the rigours of the research. But you have done an outstanding job. The report is perfect."

Janaki's face glowed with pride at his praise. Raghunath was never the one to hand out praise for the sake of it, this much she had learnt in the past month about him.

"I couldn't have done this without you," she replied.

"Well, as a mark of gratitude, you will have to treat me to coffee and samosa in the canteen," he teased, his eyes twinkling.

"Hmmm, how about coffee for you and tea for me and samosas for both of us?"

"Tea that you will poison with three heaping spoons of sugar?" They both burst into laughter at the running joke they had on the amount of sugar Janaki took in her tea.

The past month had diluted the hesitations and reserve in their interactions. They were now much more comfortable to speak their minds. However, certain boundaries still remained. They never talked about their personal lives or the fact, that whenever they were together, the world seemed a happier place.

The laughter soon faded as they looked at each other. Raghunath couldn't take his eyes off Janaki's. It seemed as if they were speaking the words that her lips couldn't. Janaki too looked unable to look away. Their attraction for each other pulsed like a living entity between them.

A raucous laughter from the corridor snapped them back to reality. Janaki looked away, her eyes shuttering the secrets of her heart again. Opening her bag, she placed the project papers inside and withdrew a gaily covered gift. Sliding it across the table to Raghunath, she said, "Thank you, Raghunath, for your help."

Raghunath opened his mouth to refuse, but anticipating his reaction, Janaki shook her head. "Please don't say no. I know this project ate away your personal time. Let me express my gratitude."

Raghunath looked away from Janaki to the small packet on the table between them. He didn't want to see gratitude in Janaki's eyes. He wanted to see some other emotion that he couldn't define himself.

Without lifting his head, he gruffly replied, "Wishing you all the best."

He heard a rustle as Janaki picked up her bag and stood up. For a few minutes she stood silently next to the table waiting for Raghunath to look up, but Raghunath kept his eyes fixed on the table.

With a soft sigh, she turned away. Raghunath felt his shoulders slump as each step took Janaki further away from him.

The magical interlude was over. There was no longer any excuse to meet or talk to Janaki.

He picked up the packet Janaki had given him and walked out of the library, his steps slow. It felt as if there was no purpose left in his life.

V

ॐ

Two separate divided silences,
Which, brought together, would find loving voice.

ॐ

The clatter of dishes from the kitchen interrupted Manan's story. A couple of kitchen staff were squabbling near the kitchen door. Manan got up to talk to them, and Mira's eyes couldn't help but follow the lean lines of his back. Suddenly conscious that she was staring at his back, she averted her eyes to glance out the window. It was already dusk. Engrossed in the tale, she had not realised the time flying by.

As Manan returned to the table, Mira felt her heart thump faster. The quiet strength he exuded made her want to know more about him.

Was this how Raghunath felt about Janaki? The feeling that something connects you to a person even though you know nothing about them.

"Sorry Mira, there is an issue with the supplies. I need to sort it out."

Mira felt disappointment wash over her upon hearing Manan's words. She really wanted to know Raghunath's story.

"Oh! If you are free, can we meet tomorrow so I can hear the rest of the story?" she asked, slinging her bag over her shoulder.

Manan looked at the kitchen door, where his assistant waited for him. He nodded to let him know he was coming. Turning to Mira, he said, "Let's do one thing. Let's meet for breakfast tomorrow. It is my day off, and I can tell you the complete story, hopefully, uninterrupted by kitchen emergencies."

"Your home?" Mira couldn't help but repeat, surprised at how casual Manan sounded, inviting her to his home.

"Yes, you know, a place with four walls and a roof," came the dry response.

Mira gave a nervous chuckle. "No, it's just that a home is a private place. Wouldn't the rest of your family mind you inviting a stranger home?"

"*Dadu* is my only family, and I think he considers you as his friend," he replied, his gaze on her.

Still, Mira hesitated.

"Look, I promise to behave myself and give you a good breakfast. I will make only a few snarky comments about your curiosity," he drawled. The twinkle in his eye invited Mira to throw caution to the winds. She knew Manan was still a stranger, but for once, she wanted to take a risk.

"Sure! Why not?" she mumbled, trying to control the nerves that were making her fingers clutch the strap of her bag.

A slow smile spread across Manan's face as he held out a hand. Still befuddled by Manan's breakfast invitation, it took Mira a few seconds to realise he wanted her to shake hands. Flushing, she placed her hand in his. His hand was warm and firm.

"I think you are staying at the Sharma's homestay? Sharma Uncle knows our address. Just follow his directions. See you tomorrow!" Giving her fingers a slight squeeze, he walked away into the kitchen.

Mira stared at the closed kitchen door, her senses tingling as the enormity of what she had agreed to hit her. *Had she just agreed to meet Manan for breakfast? At his home?*

Walking back to the homestay under the twinkling stars, Mira barely noticed the quiet of the night. Her thoughts were in a whirl. She kept thinking about Janaki and Raghunath. She couldn't believe one could love so deeply and wait so patiently for years. Along with it came the sound of Manan's voice narrating the story. The rich timbre of his voice that sent tiny jolts through her body.

Why was she feeling this tug of attraction towards Manan? He, who had been so rude at their first meeting. Mira had no answer. But it was part trepidation and part excitement that thrummed through her veins as she stood outside Manan's house the next morning.

It was a two-story house painted white with a sloping red roof. Hedges of bougainvillea marked its boundary. Through it, one could see a neat lawn bordered by multicoloured petunias. Near the old-fashioned iron gate was a crepe myrtle tree, full of tender green leaves.

She lifted the latch, wincing as it slipped from her hand to give a big clang. Her heart beat faster with each footstep on the gravel walkway towards the verandah that wrapped around the front of the house. She had reached the steps that led into the verandah when the door opened, and Raghunath stepped out.

"I thought I heard the gate. Good morning, *beta ji.* Welcome to our home," he called out.

Her nerves abated a little by the kindness in Raghunath's smile. Mira replied, "Good morning, Uncle!"

Noticing a stack of books under his arm, she asked, "Do you want to read outside in the sun? Shall I put a chair on the lawn?"

Patting his books, Raghunath said, "No *beta ji,* I already had my breakfast. I am off to the library and then to the coffeehouse. Manan is in the kitchen. Go save your breakfast before he burns it."

Chuckling at his wit, he walked down the gravel path and onto the mountain road, leaving Mira undecided at the front door.

Her nerves were back in full force.

Walk in? Just like that? Apparently yes, if Uncle was to be believed.

Taking a deep breath as she walked into the house. The main door opened into a corridor. On one side, Mira could see the living room. She continued walking straight ahead, crossing a stairwell leading to the first floor, until the end of the corridor opened into a sunny kitchen. A bank of windows overlooking the garden flanked one wall. A small table, set for breakfast for two was in front of it. In the middle of the room was a kitchen table that doubled as a prep area.

There is something to be said about a man who cooks, Mira thought, as she watched Manan deftly chop onions at the kitchen table. For once, he was wearing jeans and a form-fitting T-shirt instead of the formal trousers and button-down shirts he wore in the cafe. A lock of hair had fallen on his forehead and Mira's hands itched to brush it back. Oblivious to her standing in the doorway, Manan moved on to chopping the green chillis.

Swallowing her nerves, Mira decided to brazen it out. "Are you trying to cook breakfast or poison me?" She said, pointing at the pile of chilis on the chopping board.

Immediately, Manan's head lifted, his piercing gaze finding hers. Shooting her a crooked smile, he said, "Maybe that is my ulterior motive. Tomorrow the newspaper will carry the news. Unsuspecting tourist murdered over breakfast. The culprit poisoned her with chilis!"

Mira chuckled at the absurdity.

"So, no chillis?" he asked.

Mira shook her head, walking further into the kitchen.

"But I hope you do eat eggs? I make a mean omelette."

"Yes, I do eat them. And someone is quite confident about their cooking abilities," Mira teased.

"What can I say? Confidence has seeped into my bones," he retorted.

That certainly was true, Mira mused. The man did seem to have confidence bred into the bones. It was evident in the way he moved, the deep baritone of his voice and the straight lines of his body. He was sure of his place in the world.

It is because of his roots, to this place and Raghunath Uncle. I am a nomad, with no family and no place to call home. Shaking off the depressing thought, she asked, "May I help you?"

"Can you make the toast?" he said, whisking the onions in the eggs.

Mira moved to the counter where a cheery yellow toaster stood in all its glory. She swallowed a laugh. Never would she have guessed Manan to be a person who had a yellow toaster. She arched a look at him.

Understanding her look, Manan grinned, "Not my choice, *Dadu's.* He thought it added a splash of colour to the kitchen. I told him his design tastes matched those of a nineteen-fifties housewife."

Mira chuckled, placing two slices in the toaster before turning to Manan. Manan added the eggs to the skillet. As the eggs sizzled, he asked, "Did you have a good night's sleep?"

"Not really. I kept thinking about Raghunath and Janaki," she replied, before mentally adding, *and you.*

"I guess it is the story that dragged you here early morning, and not the charm of my company," Manan teased, amusement coating his voice.

A faint colour rose in Mira's cheeks. She was unsure how to handle this version of Manan, so different from the surly person she had met in the café.

"Of course, I came for the story. Your charms have been nonexistent till now!" she retorted, proud that her voice was steady, despite her heartbeat picking up the pace.

He walked closer to where she was. Even though he was mindful of her personal space, he was close enough for her to get a whiff of his spicy cologne. Locking his eyes with hers, his arms reached behind to pick a spatula from the holder behind her. His eyes are still intent on hers, he drawled, "And here I thought we had a connection. Such a pity!"

But before she could figure out the meaning of his words and actions, his voice turned brisk again as he moved back to the hob and said, "Anyway, let me satisfy your curiosity and continue Raghunath and Janaki's story."

VI

Raghunath sat at the desk, drumming his fingers, his eyes fixed on the silver crescent as it journeyed through the dark sky. A flickering light bulb illuminated his modest bedroom with a single bed, a desk, and a cupboard full of books. The hands of the wall clock showed it was past ten. Sleep was playing truant.

His mind was on the gift Janaki had handed in the library. He had opened it the moment he reached the privacy of his home, stunned to see it was an expensive leather-bound anthology of poems. He placed it on his desk, trying to ignore it, but like a magnet, it called to him.

Under normal circumstances, having received a new book, he would have been halfway through it. But these were not normal circumstances. He had yet to even open the book. He couldn't understand the reason for his hesitation. Was it because this was the first and possibly the last time Janaki would give him anything?

The silent hoot of the owl brought his eyes back to the book. He could not postpone it any longer.

Taking a deep breath, he opened the cover page.

"Dear Raghunath,

Thank you for your help with the project.

Janaki."

Raghunath read the inscription on the flyleaf written in Janaki's elegant handwriting. Despondency grew as he traced the words. His fingers lingered over Janaki. Shaking his head, he rifled through the pages, coming to an abrupt stop as his eyes fell on Elizabeth Barrett Browning's *If Thou Must Love Me.*

He softly whispered its words,

But love me for love's sake, that evermore

Thou mayst love on, through love's eternity.

Closing the book, he leaned back in his chair, looking at the damp stain on the ceiling. The words repeated in his mind. He felt as if it was Janaki speaking these words to him.

Your obsession with Janaki is getting out of hand, his brain warned. *But what if the book is a sign?* His heart argued.

Leaning forward, he read the words again, *love me for love's sake.*

Love, his lips formed the words as he closed his eyes. An image of Janaki popped up, sitting in the library, smiling at him. His heart thundered in his ear as an epiphany struck him.

He loved Janaki! Joy suffused his soul as he caressed the book.

No! This is wrong! His brain objected. *She is married to someone else!*

Clutching his head, Raghunath groaned. He needed to get over Janaki.

But she gave you a gift. That means she feels something for you, his heart whispered.

His face hardened as he reached a decision. There was only one way out of this emotional minefield. He needed to talk to Janaki. He knew it was not fair to her, but at this moment, he needed to say his feelings to her to get her out of his system.

*****

The other students milled around Raghunath, laughing and chattering, but he was oblivious to everyone. His entire attention was on finding Janaki. Not seeing her under the neem tree where she usually talked to her friends before classes, he decided to check in the library. He found her there, reading at one of the alcove tables. The staccato beat from his shoes shattered the hushed atmosphere of the library as he walked toward her.

Disturbed by the noise, Janaki frowned and looked up, but seeing Raghunath, a smile bloomed on her lips.

"Hi, Janaki! Thank you for the book. I wanted to discuss something important. Can you come for a cup of coffee with me?" Raghunath asked gruffly.

Janaki glanced at her wristwatch. "Shall we meet later in the canteen? I have a class in ten minutes."

"Not on the campus. A friend of mine has opened a coffeehouse near the new bus stand. We can meet there at around three," Raghunath replied.

The pencil in her hand beat a rapid tattoo as she tapped it against the table, mulling his question. She was not comfortable meeting Raghunath outside of campus. If someone from her family saw her with another man outside campus, there would be a furore. She wanted to say no, but looking at the emotions playing on Raghunath's face, she knew it was important for him. She would have to take the risk.

"Can we meet at eleven? I am supposed to be home by two-thirty," she asked.

"I will meet you there."

Janaki watched Raghunath stride out of the library, puzzled. Raghunath had been brusque, almost abrupt, and yet there was an unusual sadness in his eyes.

At eleven, the bell on Sunshine Coffeehouse's door tinkled as Janaki walked in. Raghunath was already sitting at a table in the corner. Putting her bag down, Janaki took the chair across from him.

"What did you want to talk to me so urgently? And that too away from the campus? You know if my in-laws find out I am cutting classes, they will use it as an excuse to stop me from coming to college," Janaki laughed.

Raghunath did not laugh with her. Instead, his intense eyes bored into hers. "Janaki, you are married, and my engagement is in two weeks. We both are bound to someone else. But I feel a connection with you, as if you are under my skin. Whenever I think about you, there is this constant ache in my heart."

Taking a deep breath, Raghunath plunged in, "Janaki, I love you."

Janaki's smile had faded with each word of Raghunath's impassioned speech. She sat stunned for a few minutes before rushing out of the cafe with a soft cry.

"Janaki!" called Raghunath.

Snatching the bag she had forgotten, Raghunath rushed to follow her.

Blinded by tears of anger, Janaki walked up the road into the forest. "How could he say this?" she muttered, stumbling through the trees.

"Janaki! Janaki! Please stop!" Raghunath called from behind.

Janaki ignored his pleas, continuing to walk faster, deeper into the forest.

"Janaki! Stop! I am sorry!" shouted Raghunath again.

Janaki came to an abrupt stop. Whirling around, she gave vent to her feelings. "I thought you were my friend Raghunath. How could you do this to me?"

Anger and hurt mingled, causing her voice to waver.

Raghunath came closer, pain etched on the lines of his face. "I am sorry Janaki. I didn't mean to hurt you. But I just couldn't keep my feelings to myself anymore."

"So, you decided to dump them on me?" she shouted. "What do you expect from me? That I will also profess my love for you? Is that what you want?"

Raghunath's heart leaped.

"Do you?" he asked softly.

"Do I what?" Janaki asked, exasperated.

"Do you also love me, Janaki?" Raghunath asked firmly.

"And what if I do Raghunath? How will professing my love help us? We are bound to others. We can never be together," she replied, despair coating her voice as tears fell unabashedly.

Unable to control himself, he rushed forward, taking Janaki in his arms. Her hands lifted to Raghunath's shoulders as if to push him away, but instead, stayed there, her fingers clutching the folds of his shirt.

"Hush, my love!" he whispered, holding her like a fragile doll.

Imperceptibly, degree by degree, Janaki softened against him. The distance between them reduced until her head rested on his chest. Her tears flowed at the impossibility of their situation and Raghunath let her cry, murmuring soft endearments. When the tears had run their course, Janaki lifted her face, eyes swollen.

With red-rimmed eyes, she spoke softly, "Raghunath, our words are useless. Our situation is hopeless. There is no future for us."

Raghunath caressed her cheeks, wiping away her tears with soft fingers.

"I love you," he murmured. "And that is my truth. I cannot imagine a day without seeing you. I cannot survive in a world without you in it. Our society and rituals bound you to someone else, but I believe, in our hearts, we are bound to each other."

"I refuse to cheat on my husband. Even in my dreams, I cannot think of being with you," Janaki cried, freeing herself from Raghunath's arms.

"You would deny what we have between us?" Raghunath asked in anger, moving closer to Janaki.

Taking her hand, he drew her closer.

"Do you deny that your heart longs for me? The thrill that runs through me whenever you are near me? Your heart's desire that taints your cheeks whenever I come close to you?"

His voice grew softer with each word, seducing her. Ensnared, Janaki let him draw her closer until she was in his arms again.

"My love," Raghunath whispered, looking into Janaki's warm brown eyes. Passion and desire sparkled along with tears.

Feeling as if he was in a dream, Raghunath dipped his head, pressing a soft kiss on her quivering lips. His blood sang with joy as she tentatively kissed him back. After a few moments, Janaki broke the kiss. Sighing softly, she rested her head on Raghunath's shoulder, his arms cocooning her.

They stayed like that, oblivious to the passing of time, savouring the pleasure of being with each other. Raghunath felt contentment wash over him. He loved Janaki, and Janaki loved him. This was what his heart had longed for. He didn't need anything else.

And then the peace was shattered. Janaki started speaking.

"My husband is in the army. He is a decent man. Our parents fixed our match, but in his own way, he cares for me. My in-laws are very conservative. They objected to me continuing my education after marriage. He made them understand that my education is as important as my handling of the household. He listens to what I say and doesn't ignore me. Yes, I do not love him, but I do respect him."

Raghunath opened his mouth to speak, but Janaki placed her hand over his mouth.

"No, my love, we cannot be selfish. I have two younger unmarried sisters. What do you think their marriage prospects will be if I listen to my heart and become one with you? Nor can I hurt my husband, who has been so kind. And that innocent girl, whom your mother has chosen for you, don't you think you are being unfair to her as well?"

"You will think of everyone else, but happily break my heart?" Raghunath cried out in anger.

"And mine too, Raghunath," Janaki replied softly. "Yes! I will admit I love you, but one of us needs to be practical enough to know that what we have between us needs to end now. Our union will only bring misery to those who care about us. It is not easy to bury our feelings, but we must. For the sake of our families."

"Give me something. Even a morsel of your love will help me live," Raghunath implored, trying to pull her closer as she moved away, uncaring of his ego and his pride.

Janaki shook her head, her eyes shadowed with sadness.

"Goodbye, Raghunath," she whispered, freeing herself and picking up her bag.

Helpless, Raghunath fell on his knees as he watched her walk away, her spine straight.

He hoped. He prayed. But she didn't stop. She didn't turn back to give him another glance as she disappeared through the trees. Rooted to the spot, Raghunath knelt there until the cawing of the crows heralded the approaching dusk.

With a weary heart, he walked back home.

VII

I love you now until I die
For I must love because I live
And in me is what you give.

Sunbeams danced on the dining table strewn with the remains of their breakfast. A mynah chirped in the garden outside, breaking the silence in the kitchen as Manan paused to take a sip of water. Mira gave a long sigh, rubbing a hand over her chest.

"This was so remarkably sad," she whispered.

"Yes," replied Manan. "If Janaki had shown some spine, *Dadu* would have had a happier life."

"How can you blame Janaki?" Mira asked, incredulous at Manan's lack of sympathy for Janaki's moral dilemma. "It is easy to be selfish and take what you want without thinking of anyone else. It takes a lot of courage to think and act for others."

"You think she was brave in breaking *Dadu's* heart?" Manan scorned. "Tell me, what would you have done if it had been you instead of Janaki?"

"Most probably, I would have taken the same decision as Janaki," replied Mira.

"You would not have fought for love?" Manan asked.

His gaze pierced her, almost like he wanted to look into her soul. Mira felt flustered. She felt as if Manan was testing her. Mira gave a shaky laugh.

"It is not about me, is it? It is Janaki and Uncle's story. What happened next? Why does Uncle wait at the coffeehouse every day?"

For a moment, Manan was silent, his gaze steady on Mira. And then he started speaking again.

*****

It was past eight when Raghunath reached home. He had wandered in the forest aimlessly, his heart throbbing with pain, not knowing what to do next. He knew enough about Janaki to know that she would not budge from her decision. She looked frail and petite, but she had a core of steel.

But did his life have any purpose without her?

"Where have you been? I have been waiting for you for the past hour!" asked a voice.

Shaken out of the thoughts that swirled in his mind, Raghunath looked up to see his mother sitting on the bed. Petite and always dressed in a white saree, his mother reminded whoever looked at her as a benign old lady. But Raghunath knew that the truth was quite the opposite. His mother ruled their household with an iron fist wrapped in a velvet glove.

"Nothing, Ma. I had gone for a walk after work to clear my head."

"I wanted to go saree shopping for *bahu*, but all the shops will be closed by now. Make sure you come early tomorrow. We need to start preparing for the engagement. It is only a few weeks away," she said.

Raghunath nodded instinctively, not registering his mother's words. Patting his shoulder, she left the room as Raghunath lay down on the bed, staring at the ceiling.

The next evening at the saree shop, as his mother selected sarees for the bride-to-be, the chaos of fabrics and colours jolted Raghunath awake from his indecision. He realized the meaning of Janaki's words.

If he got engaged, he would be cheating on the innocent girl, who probably would already be weaving dreams of matrimonial bliss. He, who deeply, passionately, and illogically, loved another. And wouldn't a marriage to someone else be cheating on Janaki too?

No, he decided, he couldn't do that to Janaki.

*****

The next morning, Raghunath woke up with a clear head. The fog that had engulfed him after Janaki spurned him had finally lifted. It was time to implement his decision.

Walking into the kitchen, he found his mother preparing breakfast for the family.

"Amma, I don't want to get married. Please call the bride's side to call off the engagement," he said, without any preamble.

The cup of tea slipped from his mother's surprised hands, smashing into smithereens.

"What!" she shrieked. "The engagement is less than two weeks away. I just spent a hundred rupees on five sarees yesterday and now you are saying break it off!"

Impassively, Raghunath stared back at her.

Flabbergasted, she asked, "But why? I asked you before we said yes to the girl's parents. They are ready to give money for your trip to America, plus gold. What has made you go back on your word?"

"I just don't want to get married," Raghunath replied, his voice firm.

"If you didn't want to get married, you should have said so earlier. It is too late now. What will the society and our relatives say?"

"I don't care what the people say. It is my life, and I have decided I do not want to get married."

"And what about me? What about all the sacrifices I made so that you could study without interruptions? All your childhood friends are already earning, but I never nagged you to get a job. I knew you had dreamt of doing a PhD. Now when I was getting rewards for my sacrifices, by getting a daughter-in-law to take care of me, you want to take it away!" she fumed.

Raghunath let her vent her fury in words that wounded his heart. But soon she realized that neither her words nor her tears would change Raghunath's decision. Defeated, she shut herself in her room, refusing to look at him. Ignoring her emotional blackmail, Raghunath left for college.

He needed to talk to Janaki. She had told him her decision. It was now time for her to listen to him.

****

Predictably, Raghunath found Janaki in the library. She was at the desk she usually sat, but her attention was not on the book. She was staring at the wall in front of her, her eyes unfocused.

Raghunath's heart lurched looking at her so lost and alone. He wanted to gather her in his arms, to protect her from pain. Steeling his heart against the traitorous thought, he walked closer.

Janaki's eyes widened in alarm when she noticed him. Her eyes darted around to see if someone was observing them, but she couldn't control the telltale blush rising on her cheeks.

"What are you doing here?" she whispered, "I thought I made it clear that we will not meet anymore!"

"Come with me to the coffeehouse. We need to talk," Raghunath said, ignoring her words.

"No!" Janaki said, "We said what needed to be said. There is nothing more."

"You told me your decision," Raghunath retorted. "It is my turn now!"

Janaki shook her head.

"Janaki!" Raghunath's tone warned her that he was ready to create a scene.

Looking into Raghunath's eyes, Janaki's shoulders softened.

"Fine! But only for ten minutes. I cannot risk my family finding out that I have been meeting you alone out of campus," she replied sharply.

Raghunath's thunderous expression gave away the hurt her words had caused. "Yes, I know your curfew is two thirty in the afternoon," he sneered.

Janaki's face flushed with anger at Raghunath's words, but she refrained from replying. Slinging her bag on her shoulder, she said, "Let's get this over with!"

The coffeehouse was empty when they reached. Walking to the corner table, they sat opposite each other, eyeing each other warily. Raghunath clenched his fists, fighting for control. He didn't want to do anything stupid like hold her hand or kiss her. Hurtful words might have passed between them, but like a steady flame, desire still throbbed underneath.

Clearing his throat, Raghunath started speaking.

"You told me you will not cheat on your husband. Even though you love me, you feel bound to that person. You also reminded me that I am about to be engaged. I realized that would mean cheating on you, so I have called off my marriage. The engagement was not yet done, so hopefully, this will not affect marriage prospects of the girl my mother selected for me."

Janaki made a noise as if to speak, but Raghunath shook his head, stopping her.

"Let me finish, please. I will not create a moral quandary for you. I will respect your decision to stay with your husband. I will not meet you or pester you to talk to me anymore. I only ask one thing from you. You will not object to me loving you from afar.

"I will come here every morning at eleven. You are, of course, under no compulsion to come. But, if you love me, you will come. You don't need to talk or even sit with me. Just let me look at you, know that you are fine. My only truth is that I love you. And if one day you decide to be brave and take your happiness into your own hands, I will be here waiting for you."

Raghunath looked at his watch.

"I believe my ten minutes are up. Goodbye Janaki, I will always love you!"

Without a backward glance, Raghunath walked out, leaving Janaki alone.

*****

"And that is why Uncle waits for her every day at eleven!" Mira asked incredulously. "Did she come even once?"

Manan smiled at the eagerness in Mira's voice.

"Janaki did not come to the coffeehouse for the next two months, though *Dadu* waited every day. But then, one day, Janaki came. She would come at eleven, always taking the table where they could see each other. They didn't speak, or even acknowledge each other, but just looked at each other. She would leave at noon.

"*Dadu* didn't know what excuse she gave at home, but every day she was there, just like he was, to catch a glimpse of her love. This continued for about six months. And then, one day, just as suddenly, she stopped coming. And *Dadu* has been waiting for her ever since."

Mira looked at the rose bush sway in the breeze from the kitchen window as Manan came to the end of the tale.

"You said Uncle broke off the match his mother had fixed, so whom did he marry?" Mira asked, looking back at Manan.

"No one," replied Manan.

"But you call Uncle *Dadu*?" Mira asked, puzzled.

"That's a story for another day. I need to go to the coffeehouse to meet *Dadu*," Manan said, looking at his watch.

Getting up, he casually added, "Will you walk with me to the coffeehouse?"

Mira nodded. Picking up her bag, she opened her mouth to ask another question when Manan said, "Shush! Save the questions. I am tired of telling *Dadu*'s tale. Why don't we talk about something else?"

"Like?"

"Like, how about I apologise to you for the first day in the coffeehouse when I didn't help you with your suitcase? In my defence, I did start walking towards you to help, but you had already gotten your suitcase free before I reached the door."

Manan's sudden apology surprised Mira. Fiddling with the strap of her bag, she asked, "What made you apologise today?"

Manan walked closer, looking deep into her eyes. "I didn't want you to have a bad impression of me."

"And that matters?"

"Yes, it does."

"Why?"

"Just because...." was all he said, before his lips curved upward.

His smile is lethal, Mira thought, giving herself a mental shake. Trying to ignore how the musky notes of his cologne were making her blood fizz in delight, she took a step back, putting some distance between them.

"What do you want to talk about?" Mira asked, turning towards the door, trying to break the spell Manan was weaving with his crooked smile and intense brown eyes.

Manan shot her an amused look, as if aware of what Mira was trying to do. Matching her casual tone, he stepped in next to her. "Movies? Do you watch horror? Which is your favourite?"

Mira gave a mock shudder. "Horror? No way! My favourite movie is Andaz Apna Apna!"

"Looks like we will have to improve your repertoire of movies. Who loves Andaz Apna Apna?" scoffed Manan.

Bickering, they walked down the road that led to the town's centre.

Later that night, sitting on the balcony of her room, Mira looked at the stars and reflected upon the day gone by. Thinking about Raghunath and Janaki made her feel melancholy. They seemed to be victims of fate and societal expectations.

What would it feel like to have such steadfast love? To not be swayed by time or circumstances, surviving on the hope that the other person, one day, might come back.

Unbidden, Manan's face came up in her mind.

She had had a wonderful time with him that evening. They had discussed music and movies. He had made her chuckle with his dry one-liners. Not to mention the fact that even a whiff of his cologne made her heart thump. He had been abrasive at first, but then, she too had been a fool, asking a personal question of a stranger. It was evident that he cared deeply about Raghunath and was quite protective of him. That, honestly, made him much more attractive.

Thank God I am leaving tomorrow, or else I would have been in danger of falling in love with him, she thought, turning off the lights as her lips curved remembering his wavy hair that he wore a tad too long, eyes that seemed to look right into her soul, and a smile that made her heart flip-flop.

VIII

All thoughts, all passions, all delights,
Whatever stirs this mortal frame.

The sun felt warm on her back as Mira dragged her suitcase into the coffeehouse. She waved to Raghunath who was seated at his regular table in the back. Leaving the suitcase next to the door, she went to talk to him.

"Good morning, *beta ji*! Where are you going?" Raghunath asked, pointing towards her suitcase.

Mira's smile dimmed a little. "Holidays are over. I have to join back tomorrow."

"So soon?"

Mira shrugged. "Even getting this time off was so difficult. Don't you remember? My boss gave me work?"

Raghunath patted her hand gently. "It is my fault. I had forgotten that you were here only for a few days. I have grown quite fond of you!"

Impulsively Mira reached over and hugged him. "Me too, Uncle. I wish I didn't have to go. I will miss you and the coffeehouse while struggling with deadlines. Why don't you give me your phone number and I will call you?"

"*Beta ji*, I told you before, I don't have a mobile. But I will give you my landline number. I am always at home in the evenings."

"And here is my number," Mira said, handing over her visiting card to Raghunath. "You can also call me whenever you want."

Just then, Manan came over carrying two cups of coffee.

Turning towards him, Raghunath announced, "Mira is leaving today."

Manan looked at Mira with hooded eyes, "Holidays are over?"

"Yes, I have to join tomorrow," Mira replied softly, wondering if there was a hint of reproach she heard in his voice.

"What time is your bus? I will walk down to the bus stop with you," Manan said.

"It is ok. I am not going by bus. I have booked a cab. It should be here any moment now," she replied.

As if on cue, her phone pinged.

"The driver is here," Mira announced, looking at the message that had popped up.

She gave a watery smile to Raghunath and a quick goodbye to Manan before turning and walking out of the café.

She could feel Manan's eyes on her back, but Mira knew she couldn't turn back. If she did, the tears she had somehow managed to control would brim over.

The heaviness in her heart felt more than the regular post-holiday blues. She hated that she couldn't walk through the winding streets to the coffeehouse and chat with Raghunath about books every morning. That she wouldn't be able to sneak glances at Manan and admire the way he managed the café. Efficient, yet with a hint of warmth.

The whole drive back to the city, Mira cursed herself for the stilted conversation with Manan. She wished she had told him to stay in touch, she wished she had given him her number or asked him for his.

It is just a crush. I will grow out of it, she consoled herself, unlocking the door to her modest flat. It was time to get back to real life.

*****

Spring turned to summer, and summer turned to monsoon. The seasons whirled by as Mira got sucked into the hamster wheel of meetings and deadlines. During her free moments, her thoughts would wander to Raghunath and Manan. Many times, she almost called Raghunath but stopped. She knew Manan's name would crop up in the conversations with Raghunath.

She was not sure if she was over her crush on Manan and wanted to talk about him. Even now whenever she would lie down to sleep, Manan's smiling face would pop up unbidden, causing a funny sensation in her heart.

She quashed any thoughts of calling Raghunath by giving herself the excuse of pending work.

*****

It was one of the days that Mira wanted over before it even began. The heavens had decided to dump an entire week's rain in one day on the city. There was no Uber to be found which meant Mira had to survive a hair-raising auto ride to the office.

The *autowallah*, like *autowallas* all over the country, ignored her pleading to drop her under the portico. He dropped her off at the main gate, which meant she had to walk in the pouring rain, battling the wind to keep the umbrella on her head. Her woes continued once she reached the relative safety of her office building. The umbrella decided it was now time to play and refused to close.

"When will this day get over!" she muttered, struggling to close her dripping umbrella. A drop of water found its way into her collar, rolling down her back and making her shoulders itch.

"Mira!" a voice called out.

Mira whirled around. The frown on her face was quickly replaced by surprise. Her eyes widened as Manan strode through the crowd towards her.

"Hi, Mira!" he said, stopping a few steps away. A little smile hovered over his lips.

Unable to believe Manan was standing in front of her, the first words out of Mira's mouth were, "What are you doing here?"

Manan's smile faded upon hearing her brusque tone. The earlier warmth of his voice was missing as he replied, "We are revamping the coffeehouse. I came to the town to buy some new dishware. When I told *Dadu* I was coming to the city, he gave me your visiting card and insisted I meet you. But I think this was a mistake."

Manan turned to walk away. Dropping the dripping umbrella on the floor, Mira rushed to stop him.

"Manan, stop! I didn't mean to sound unwelcoming. I am just...gobsmacked seeing you here. Shall we grab a cup of coffee? And did you say something about revamping the coffeehouse?" She asked, giving him a bright smile, hoping he would stay.

Manan looked at her for a few minutes before looking at his watch. "My cab is waiting outside as I have a few appointments. I just wanted to come and say hello first. Are you free for dinner tonight?"

Mira nodded.

"Great! *Dadu* gave me your mobile number. Is it ok if I send you a text message? You can send me your address location and I will pick you up?"

Befuddled, Mira could once again only nod.

With a quick wave, Manan walked out of the lobby. Mira watched as he disappeared in the crowds of office workers, unable to believe what had just happened.

Her heart felt it would soar away with delight. She had met Manan, and they were going to have dinner together. It was almost as if her dreams had manifested him here. A bump from a co-worker made her come back to reality.

With a giddy giggle, she joined the queue for the lift. She just couldn't wait for the working hours to get over, she had a dinner to go to!

*****

Mira paced the living room, her stomach full of butterflies. Anticipation for the evening had made focusing on work difficult. Finally, she had punched out a couple of hours early.

Mira didn't know if Manan was attracted to her, but she didn't want to lose this opportunity to impress him. She wanted to look attractive but confident.

She agonised over an hour about what to wear, changing her outfit five times before finally settling on a white sleeveless blouse and a pair of figure-hugging jeans. Sparkly sneakers completed her look. She draped a denim jacket over her shoulders to avoid catching a cold in the nippy weather. Nude lipstick and barely-there eyeliner completed her look. Looking at her reflection, she gave a satisfied nod. All she had to do now was wait and make sure the butterflies didn't come streaming out her throat when she opened her mouth.

The butterflies fluttered faster as the doorbell chimed. Taking a calming breath, she opened the door to see Manan. He held a bouquet of yellow roses in his hand.

"Oh! How lovely!" Mira gushed as he handed it to her.

"Please come in. Let me put them in a vase before we leave. Otherwise, they will wilt," she said, her eyes bright with pleasure.

Manan stepped in, his eyes taking her tiny, but neat, open-planned living room. A breakfast bar, that doubled up as a dining table, separated the kitchen from the living area. The living area had an L-shaped couch, with multi-coloured cushions facing the TV hung on the opposite wall.

But Manan's attention was taken up by a huge bookcase that ran through one end of the room. A well-worn armchair covered by an embroidered throw stood in front of it. Next to the armchair was a small round table piled high with books and a photograph of a couple.

He walked closer to inspect the photo.

"My parents," Mira said, walking into the living area, the vase in her hands. "I lost them when I was in university."

Vase still in hand she went to stand next to him. Her smile was tinged with sadness as she gestured to the armchair. "The chair was my father's, and the throw had been embroidered by my mother for one of their anniversaries."

He looked at her, noticing the sheen in her eyes, "You miss them a lot."

She gave a half-shrug, "I do, but then I look at this apartment I bought from the savings they left me. I use the objects that were theirs. All of it makes me feel as if they are still around, taking care of me."

They were quiet for a moment before Mira gave herself a little shake to get rid of the melancholy.

Turning to Manan, she asked, "Did you like my apartment?"

"Do you seriously want to know, or are you making small talk?"

"I want to know." Mira was not surprised that it was the truth. What Manan felt about her apartment, which had so much of her in it, would give her an idea of how he thought about her.

Putting his hands in his pockets, he nodded, half-turning to survey the room. "It tells a lot about you," he replied.

"Oh really? Like what?" she asked, her brow arched.

"That you like reading and colours," he said, gesturing to the cushions on her sofa.

"I think colours add joy to our lives," she replied.

"They certainly do," he murmured, glancing at her blue jacket contrasting with the yellow roses in her hand.

The space between them seemed to shrink as they stared at each other.

The spell was broken by the pinging of Manan's phone. He glanced away, to look at his watch. "Shall we leave? Else we will be late for our booking," he asked.

Unable to speak, Mira nodded, rushing to place the vase on the dining table.

Control yourself! It is just dinner; she scolded herself, following Manan out of the apartment.

IX

ജ

Tell me dearest what is love?
'Tis a lightening from above.

ജ

The deluge in the morning had chased away the humidity that usually plagued the city in the monsoon. The air was cool and fresh, as Mira walked with Manan to the restaurant. There was a lightness in her spirits, which had been missing ever since she had returned from the hills. The reason could be the weather, or it might have to do with the fact that she was with Manan.

Manan had picked a good restaurant for dinner. It was near her apartment so they could walk and enjoy the weather, the staff was attentive without being pretentious, and the music was loud enough to be heard, but not to make conversation impossible. It was, in fact, a perfect place for a casual dinner between friends. And yet, as Mira took a fortifying sip of her wine, sneaking a look at Manan, an awkward silence sat like a third wheel on their table.

Manan kept his eyes fixed on the basket of bread the server had placed on the table, while Mira hid behind the menu, trying to decide the mains and secretly admiring how Manan's black shirt stretched across his shoulders.

Enough with drooling over Manan! You are out on dinner with the fellow. Talk to him! She reminded herself as her brain searched for topics to kickstart their conversation. The moment they seemed to have shared in her apartment, seemed to have put a bump in the easy interaction earlier.

Coffeehouse! Yes, that was a safe topic.

"You mention you are revamping the coffeehouse? Tell me more about it?" she asked.

Her arrow hit home as Manan's face lit up with a smile. "Yes. It was Sunita's idea. She felt that the decor could do with some updating. The colour scheme of the interiors needed freshness. I have a list of furniture, dishware, and light fixtures I am supposed to buy in the city. She has also given me the specific names of the stores I need to buy from. But most importantly, we are rebranding it as Cafe Sunshine."

Seeing the animation on Manan's face as he talked about Sunita, Mira felt her heart wobble.

Was Sunita someone special? Keeping her voice deliberately casual, Mira asked, "Who is Sunita?"

"Oh, I guess you didn't meet Sunita. She wasn't in town when you came for your holiday. Sunita is the only daughter of Mr. Kailash Sharma, a reputed business owners in our town. She studied abroad and has been of great help in organising everything. The rebranding is also her idea. She says Cafe Sunshine will work better with the youngsters who come to our town for holidays."

And I bet Sunita is nubile and beautiful too! Mira thought uncharitably, buttering a roll. "Is Uncle ok with the renovation and name change?" Mira asked after she had swallowed the bread and some of her irritation at Sunita.

"It was *Dadu* who convinced me to listen to Sunita's suggestions. I would not have dreamed of changing anything without his consent anyway," Manan replied.

Et tu Uncle, Mira thought, growing more miserable by the minute, listening to Manan extol the unknown Sunita's many talents.

"But how will Janaki find Uncle if she comes? Will she be able to recognise the coffeehouse if you change it to a cafe?" Mira asked, desperate to stop Sunita's ideas from coming to fruition.

Manan looked incredulous.

"Do you really think Janaki is going to come? For far too long, *Dadu* has clung to this ridiculous hope that Janaki will come. He has waited, putting his life and career on hold for a woman who did not have the courage to fight for her love. Now that *Dadu* is ready to take a step forward, you are telling me to stop him?"

Mira felt her ears burn at the anger in Manan's voice but refused to back down.

"Stranger things have happened, Manan. Even if there is a minuscule chance that Janaki might come back, then there is still hope. Sacrifices made in the course of love are worthwhile in the arms of the beloved."

Manan shook his head.

"Never thought a girl who lives in the big city could be such a daft romantic! And anyway, why do you care so much?"

Mira bristled at the scorn in his tone. Leaning forward in her chair, she ground out, "What do you mean by a daft romantic? And why shouldn't I care about Raghunath Uncle? He was kind to me. He is my friend!"

"Friend? Whom you didn't call even once in the past six months?" Manan retorted.

Mira deflated on hearing these words. In a softer tone, she said, "I miss him. And yes, it is true that even though I wanted to, I didn't call him."

"Why Mira? Do you know how attached he got in the short time that you were there? He wanted to call you but refrained, as he thought you might be busy. He assumed you would call whenever you were free. But you never did. When he came to know that I was coming to the city, he made me promise I would meet you. Even when I didn't want to."

Mira flinched at the accusation in Manan's words, but his last sentence pierced her heart. She couldn't control her emotions anymore.

"Because of you!" she cried, giving her emotions a free rein. "I would have called Uncle, but invariably he would have talked about you. I didn't want to talk about you!"

The moment they had left Mira's lips, she wished she could take them back.

The silence after her outburst was deafening. They stared at each other as a flush rose in both their cheeks.

Manan was the first to break the silence. In a calm voice, contrasting with the vein that throbbed at his temple, he said, "I apologize, Mira. I didn't know you wanted to avoid meeting or talking to me. I would not have come to your office or invited you for dinner, if I had known my presence was abhorrent. I hope you will understand if I don't stay any longer or drop you home."

Horrified, Mira saw Manan getting up and walking out, leaving her alone. "Manan!" she called out, but he didn't stop or glance back.

That night Mira wept as she had never wept before. Her heart felt as if it had broken into a million pieces. She couldn't believe she had been thoughtless enough to tell Manan that she didn't want to talk about him without telling him why.

Mira realised it was not infatuation that had plagued her when she came back from the holiday. Somehow, in those five days, unknowingly, she had fallen in love with Manan.

X

The next morning Mira woke up with swollen eyes, a stuffy nose, and a heavier heart. She had tossed and turned the entire night, replaying the conversation with Manan, wanting to take her words back.

It was routine rather than any desire for tea that had her venturing into the kitchen. She looked at the phone as she waited for the water to boil. Manan was right. By not calling Raghunath, she had hurt the man who had been nothing but kind to her. Her friendship with Raghunath needed to be independent of her feelings for Manan.

Not that he would talk to me now after what I said last night, Mira thought miserably.

She glanced at the clock. Raghunath would not have left for the coffeehouse. She scrolled through her contacts before dialing the one she was looking for. Raghunath picked up the phone on the fourth ring.

Mira could hear the pleasure in his voice when he said, "*Beta ji!* So nice of you to call me. I have been waiting to talk to you."

Mira's heart gave a guilty twinge on hearing his words. With cheerfulness that she didn't feel, she said, "Sorry Uncle, for not having called. But I am upset with you too. Why didn't you call me? You still consider me a tourist in your town and not your friend, right?"

Raghunath laughed at her emotional blackmail. "You certainly know how to turn the tables on this old man, my dear. I get your point. From now on, I will not wait but call you whenever I feel like talking to you. Now tell me, how is everything? Did you meet Manan?"

Mira's smile dimmed, and her heart clenched hearing Manan's name as she remembered her words to him.

Trying to keep her voice even, she said, "Yes, Uncle, I met Manan yesterday. I was surprised to hear that the coffeehouse is being renovated."

"It was time for a change, *beta ji*," Raghunath said calmly. Before Mira could respond or object, he added, "Sunita is such a lovely girl. She has such good ideas. We are all very fond of her."

Mira felt irritation rising in her again.

Sunita seems to have done magic. Uncle and Manan keep repeating her name in every sentence. Not wanting to hear more about Sunita and her qualities, Mira ended the conversation by apologising that she was late for work. But before hanging up, she promised Raghunath that she would stay in touch.

As Mira got ready for work, she mused that the easier job of talking to Raghunath was done. But how could she make things right with Manan? Should she declare her feelings for him or give him an excuse as to why talking about him would be painful for her?

One thing was sure, she couldn't leave things the way they were between them. If nothing else, she did want Manan in her life as a friend.

Adulting and doing the right thing is hard, Mira mused, as she walked into her office. She needed to protect her heart, and also, safeguard Manan's feelings. *I will call him in the evening,* she decided, *and apologise for my rudeness yesterday.*

*****

By the time evening came Mira was far from feeling calm. Her mind was churning with the imaginary conversations she had been having the whole day. Practising the words she wanted to say, trying to guess what Manan's response would be. With the turmoil going on in her mind, a headache threatened, as she unlocked the door to her apartment.

After a long, hot shower, Mira knew she couldn't procrastinate any longer. It would soon be too late to call. She picked up the phone to call, but before she could do anything, it started ringing.

Manan's name flashed on the screen.

Mira's breathing quickened. Taking a deep breath, Mira pressed the answer button.

"Hello!" she said, her voice huskier than usual.

There was a slight pause from the other side before Manan's deep voice came online. "Hello, Mira. I am sorry for disturbing you this evening, but I wanted to apologize for my behaviour last night. It was rude and ungentlemanly of me to walk out and leave you alone."

Mira was stunned. Even though his tone was stilted, Manan was apologising!

Clearing her throat, Mira said, "No apology needed. I am very sorry for hurting your feelings. It was very insensitive of me to say I didn't want to talk about you. I did not mean it the way it came out. You were not to be blamed."

"Nonetheless, I was rude, and I still owe you dinner. Shall we try again today?"

Mira wished she could see Manan's expression then. *Was he asking only as a courtesy, or did he still want to have dinner with her?* Unsure, Mira stayed quiet.

The silence stretched before Manan added, "Only if you are ok with meeting me?"

Mira almost laughed out loud. *Ok with meeting Manan!* If only he knew how much she longed to see him, to be near him. *But why should she not?* Her heart questioned. This was Manan, the man she had fallen in love with. Why should she not meet him and enjoy time with him?

Taking a deep breath, she replied, "Manan, I am too tired to go out tonight."

"Oh," came his one-word reply.

"Why don't you come home? I was about to make dinner for myself. We can sit and chat. It will be payback for your bread omelette." Mira was quick to add before Manan felt rejected.

Five minutes later, Mira rushed into the kitchen. The menu for the night had changed from Maggi. She quickly made a simple pasta with a side of garlic bread before changing out of her sweatpants.

No one looking at me would realise how nervous I am, she thought forty-five minutes later, critically staring at her reflection. Her outfit of jeans and a kurta exuded casual, comfortable vibes.

Taking a scrunchy, she piled up her hair in a high ponytail and was applying lip gloss when the doorbell rang.

Putting a hand on her stomach to calm the churning within, she opened the door to see Manan standing with a cake box in his hand.

"Dessert as a peace offering," he said holding out the box. His smile was hesitant.

Mira smiled back, attraction and nervousness warring in her heart.

Their hands brushed as she took the box. Mira's eyes widened in surprise as she felt a jolt of electricity pass through her. She could see the same awareness flaring in Manan's eyes.

Eyes still locked on Manan's Mira imperceptibly swayed towards him.

The moment was broken by Manan drawling, "Static. Maybe you need to moisturize."

Unnerved by his touch and her reaction to him, Mira struggled to keep her voice casual as she replied, "Maybe."

Gesturing for Manan to enter the home, Mira walked to the breakfast bar to place the cake box, mentally thanking Manan for making that stupid asinine comment. Irritation at him for having given a personal hygiene comment had helped to get her erratic heart under control.

Offering him a glass of water, Mira decided it was best to plunge right in.

"I think I should clear the air about yesterday. I didn't mean what I said about not wanting to have a conversation with Raghunath Uncle about you."

But before she could go further, Manan held up his hand to stop her from speaking.

"It is ok, Mira. I think we both were rude yesterday. Maybe it was the workday stress or irritation, but to be honest, I do want us to be friends. Not only because you are *Dadu's* friend, but because I too need an honest friend in my life. Do you think it is possible? Can we try to be friends?"

A smile lit up Mira's face on hearing his words. "Shall we try again?" she said, waving her hand, "Hi! I am Mira."

"Hi! I am Manan," he replied, chuckling at her goofiness.

The rest of the evening flew by. Mira was surprised at how easy it was to talk to Manan once the initial hesitation had passed. They once again bickered about their choices of movies with Manan trying to persuade her to start watching horror movies.

Mira on the other hand was stunned that Manan didn't enjoy reading. "Even though Raghu Uncle is a literature professor and is rarely without a book?" She asked.

Manan shrugged in reply, the twinkle in his eye deepening as he said, "Give me a movie over a book any day. The gorier the better!"

Mira gave a mock shudder at his words before the topic once again changed.

There was nothing remotely romantic about their conversation, yet Mira spent the evening in a state of heightened awareness. She was acutely aware of his nearness. Her eyes were constantly drawn to his well-toned body. His cologne was mild and yet, seemed to tempt her senses.

It was almost eleven when they said goodbye. As Mira walked Manan to the door, he said, "Thank you, Mira, for accepting me as a friend. I am going back tomorrow. Stay in touch and I hope to see you again soon."

At Mira's nod, he smiled. His expression said he wanted to add something more. But then he shook his head. With a soft "Goodbye, Mira," he walked away.

Mira watched him striding towards the lift from the door. She wanted to stop him. To confess her love for him. But Manan had just said he was glad of her as a friend. He had given no indication, either by his words or his actions that he was romantically interested in her. Except for that fleeting brush of fingers, Manan had been careful not to invade her personal space or even touch her accidentally.

While her heart and mind argued, Manan turned around to give Mira a cheery wave, before stepping into the lift and disappearing from her view.

How does Love speak?
In the faint flush upon the telltale cheek.

"Why are you not coming for the opening of Cafe Sunshine?" Manan demanded.

Mira gave an exasperated sigh.

"When you told me the tentative date, I told you it might be difficult for me. There is a product launch the day after. I can come the weekend after, but you don't want to shift the dates."

It had been six months since Mira and Manan had last met. The day when Mira had suppressed her romantic dreams about Manan, content to remain his friend the way he wanted.

It had been six months of phone calls. Phone calls that either ended in arguments or stretched late into the night as they discussed anything and everything under the sun. It had been six months of Mira falling deeper in love and hiding it.

It had also been six months of Manan gushing over the efficiency and talent of Sunita and Mira, trying to suppress the green-eyed monster every time Manan brought up her name.

The remodelling was finally complete, and Manan unreasonably wanted Mira to drop everything to attend the grand re-launch as Sunshine Coffeehouse changed into Cafe Sunshine.

"If you valued us as friends, you would be here. You know how important it is for both of us," Manan argued.

"Don't you dare emotionally blackmail me," Mira warned, trying to rein in her temper. "I know how important the coffeehouse is, especially to Uncle. But I cannot just drop everything and come. I have a responsibility towards my job."

"So your company is more important than us," Manan retorted. "And it is no more a coffeehouse, it is a cafe! Cafe Sunshine!"

Mira rolled her eyes at his childish tantrum. With an annoyed huff, she disconnected the call before she said something unpardonably rude. She stared at the phone in her hand, pinching the bridge of her nose. Headache, induced by her argument with Manan, knocked at the base of the skull.

Manan's words had hurt her more than she cared to admit. She had a product launch to attend, but it was also true that she wanted to be with Manan and Raghu Uncle for the launch.

But a part of her was hesitant to go back. She needed to maintain a distance from Manan. Talking to him over the phone had made her fall in love with him even more. What would happen when he would be in front of her? When every emotion on his face was visible to her. When she could touch and feel him.

And would she be able to control her jealousy that she was sure would flare on seeing Sunita with him?

She still needed to figure out Manan's relationship with Sunita. Mira was still not sure if he was interested in Sunita or if he counted her as a close friend. This jealousy and pretend friendship while being head over heels in love was playing havoc with her heart and mind.

Sighing, Mira tried to bring her focus back to her work.

It was past ten in the night when Mira finally wrapped up work. Rolling her shoulders to get rid of the crick in her neck, she picked up her bag. Juggling the files in her hand, she opened Uber when her phone rang.

She groaned, seeing Manan's name flash. Mira loved the man, she truly did, but she was not blind to the fact that the man was as stubborn as a goat. She was too tired to argue why she couldn't attend the relaunch.

Swiping to take the call, she snarled, "What?"

Her exhaustion was clear in the surliness of her tone.

"I have pushed the launch date back to the weekend after," Manan said. His flat voice matched the surliness in hers. "You had better be there," he warned before disconnecting the call.

Mira stared at the phone, her mouth agape.

And then she smiled.

He had changed the dates for her. Hope sparked. Maybe Manan did care for her a little. Exhaustion forgotten Mira walked out of the office humming a tune. Only a few more days before she would be back in the hills with Raghu Uncle and Manan.

XII

Love is like the wild rose-briar,
Friendship like the holly-tree.

Thank God, it hasn't rained, thought Mira, looking at the cloudless, clear sky.

Mira's gamble of having the launch of an eco-friendly food packing brand outdoors had paid off. The weather gods seemed pleased, as barely any of the usual smog blanketed the city. One could almost see a few stars twinkle.

The decor tied in beautifully with the sustainable ethos of the product. The branches of the trees twinkled with fairy lights, and candles dotted the lawn, creating a magical atmosphere in the garden of the five-star hotel.

The influencers invited to the event were impressed, and looking at the trends, the social media frontier seemed to be conquered. With the launch such a huge success, there was no way that her boss would not give Mira the month off she had requested. Mira had decided she didn't want to go for a rushed visit to the launch of Cafe Sunshine. She wanted to spend time with Raghunath.

From the past few phone conversations with Raghunath, she had the nagging feeling that something was troubling Raghunath. Her heart said that even though Raghunath seemed to have moved on, Janaki was still in his thoughts. Though how she would spend weeks seeing Manan daily and not confess her love, she did not know. It was a battle for another day.

To distract her thoughts that turned to Manan with alarming frequency, she started clicking pictures for her personal Instagram page. She took a couple of steps back to get the lights in focus when she bumped into someone.

"I am so sorry!" she said hastily, turning to see an elderly lady into whom she had bumped.

Dressed in an ivory silk saree, pearls around her neck and discrete diamond earrings, the lady seemed to belong to a family with old money. Elegance seemed to have bred into her bones.

"Not a problem. Youngsters nowadays look more at their phones than at their surroundings." The kind smile playing on her lips took the sting out of her barb.

Mira flushed at the lady's comment but admitted it was her fault. "Sorry, you are correct. I should have checked before walking back."

The lady waved her hand towards the lit room behind, "It is ok, beta. Most people here are too busy taking pictures rather than enjoying these beautiful surroundings." She looked at Mira closely before asking, "Are you Mira Rajput?"

At Mira's surprise nod, she replied, "I am Mrs. Malhotra, Dev Malhotra's grandmother."

Mira's polite smile changed into a genuine one. "Oh! How nice to meet you, Mrs. Malhotra. I have heard quite a bit about you from Dev."

Dev Malhotra was the owner of the brand Mira had just helped launch. They had worked closely for the past few months. Mira liked Dev's easygoing style, and they both had an informal working relationship where they could be honest about their opinions.

"Good things, I hope," Mrs. Malhotra replied, her brown eyes twinkling. As they both chuckled at her statement, Dev walked up with two glasses of champagne.

If there were ever a poster boy for a Mills and Boon romance, it would be Dev Malhotra. Extremely good-looking, with hair that fell in stylish curls and dark eyes that tempted one to break the rules and indulge. But rather than his good looks, it was his cheery good humour that never cracked even under pressure that had impressed Mira.

"Ladies!" Dev said, handing them both a glass. "Mira, this launch is beyond my expectations. You have made my product the talk of the town!"

Mira smiled, pleased with his praise. "Your product deserves praise for being so innovative," she murmured.

"Don't be so modest," Mrs. Malhotra added. "Accept credit where it is due. So often, we try to brush our hard work under the carpet to appear polite. When, in truth, we should be taking pride and credit for them. Dev's product is excellent. But your hard work made sure that it started trending. Else it would have been languishing in stores. So, well done!"

Mira nodded her acknowledgement at Mrs. Malhotra's words.

"Mira, I have a proposal for you," Mrs. Malhotra added. "Would it be possible to meet for coffee tomorrow morning?"

"Of course, Mrs. Malhotra, just text me the time and place," Mira replied.

"Excellent! I will take your number from Dev and message you," Mrs. Malhotra replied. "And please call me Aunty! When you say Mrs. Malhotra, I am reminded of my mother-in-law!" she added.

Mira chuckled. "Sure, Aunty!" she replied.

A guest called out Mrs. Malhotra's name from behind. Giving the guest a cheery wave, Mrs. Malhotra gave Mira and Dev a warm smile. "Have a great evening," she said, leaving them alone.

Turning to Dev, Mira commented, "I liked your grandmother. She made me feel so comfortable even though I bumped into her. And I couldn't help but notice an aura of peace around her. She instinctively made me feel calm."

"Peace is something she had worked hard for," Dev replied cryptically, looking at his grandmother as she talked to the guests. Some nameless emotion darkened his face, surprising Mira. She had never seen such a serious countenance on him.

A laugh in the distance seemed to remind Dev of his surroundings. His face cleared, and with his customary cheerful smile, he looked at Mira and said, "A few of my friends are going for a hike next weekend. I was wondering if you would like to join us?"

Mira was surprised. Till now, Mira's relationship with Dev had been easygoing but professional. So where did the idea of meeting beyond the office hours come from? An ugly suspicion raised its head. Was Dev interested in her?

She glanced at the candles flickering in the darkness, her fingers tapping against the champagne glass. She needed to be diplomatic to avoid damaging her professional relationship with Dev.

As if understanding her reason for hesitation, Dev spoke again, "I will be honest with you. I think you are attractive, and I would like to know more about you. I was waiting until the product launch to ask you out so that our professional and personal lives don't interfere. What do you think? Shall we explore another facet of friendship between us?"

Dev's words put her on the spot, but Mira knew she needed to be honest and not lead him on.

Regretfully, Mira shook her head. "Sorry Dev. I would like to be friends with you, but beyond that, I don't think anything is possible."

"Ah well! No harm, no foul," Dev said. "Why don't you anyway come hiking with us? Strictly as friends?"

Mira shook her head again. "Sorry, but I am on vacation for a month from the weekend."

Dev smiled ruefully. "Seems it is a night of disappointment for me. Have a great vacation, Mira. Stay in touch!"

As Dev walked away, Mira felt a pang in her heart. She had involuntarily hurt a good man. It could have been so easy to fall for Dev, of even temperament, he treated her with respect and lived in the same city. But no, her heart had to fall for a surly cafe owner who refused to share his secrets with her.

XIII

Love is not love
Which alters when it alteration finds.

Mira sat at the table in the corner, looking out through the window. The buzz of the cafe behind her was like white noise as she looked at the bustling street below. Mira had been surprised when the Uber had dropped her at the address texted by Mrs. Malhotra. Perched in the by-lanes of the old city, accessible by narrow stairs, the cafe was warm and welcoming. Even though the location was quaint, the insides were modern.

Mrs. Malhotra was late for their meeting, but Mira didn't mind. The weeks leading up to Dev's product launch were hectic. It was good to enjoy some free time and let her mind wander.

A flurry at the cafe's entrance distracted Mira. A smile bloomed when she saw Mrs. Malhotra approaching.

"Thank you for meeting me," Mrs. Malhotra said, reaching out to shake Mira's hand.

"It is my pleasure. And you have chosen such a lovely place to meet. If I had refused, I would have missed visiting this hidden gem," Mira replied.

"It is warm and cosy, no?" Mrs. Malhotra replied. "It is one of my favourite places in the city."

"How did you find it?" Mira asked. "I get so busy with work that I have barely explored the city, even though I have lived here for more than six years now."

Mrs. Malhotra gave an amused laugh. "I own the cafe. I started it about fifteen years back."

Mira's eyebrows rose. "Wow? I am impressed! It is such a fabulous place. It must have been back-breaking work."

A smile played on Mrs. Malhotra's lips. "Yes, it was, but the result was absolutely worth it."

Mira could see the pride in Mrs. Malhotra's eyes as she looked at what she had built.

"What did you want to talk to me about?" Mira asked, bringing the conversation to the reason for their meeting.

"I saw the wonders you did with Dev's product. It has become the talk of the town. Could you do the same for the cafe?" Mrs. Malhotra said, offering a plate of chocolate chip cookies the server had placed on the table.

"I was lucky that my company assigned me to launch Dev's product. The cafe is already up and running. What can be my company's role now?" Mira asked, puzzled, picking up a cookie.

"As you said, the cafe is a hidden gem, but to be honest, it is not as profitable as I want it to be. I want to build its customer base," Mrs. Malhotra said.

"But Mrs. Malhotra, I do product launches, and that too when the company assigns me. This is the food industry," Mira argued. "You would have to talk to my boss about it."

"Aunty," Mrs. Malhotra corrected before continuing to convince Mira. "It is not much different from a product, is it? You have to create a buzz about the cafe, like how you did with Dev's product. I am confident enough that people will love it. The cafe just needs to be more visible," Mrs. Malhotra reasoned.

Mira shook her head. "I wish I could. Even if I say yes, I cannot start work on it immediately. I am leaving at the end of the week for a month-long holiday."

"I am in no hurry. The cafe can remain a hidden gem for another month," Mrs. Malhotra said, waving her hand. "Another request, I don't want to go through your boss. I want only you to work on the ideas for the café. Why don't you take your holiday to think it over? Who knows, you might use my cafe as a steppingstone to strike out on your own rather than work for someone else?" she added.

Mira looked thoughtfully at Mrs. Malhotra, who innocently grinned in response.

"Now, have a piece of the carrot cake. It is our best-seller," Mrs. Malhotra said, waving over a waiter.

As Mira forked a piece of the moist carrot cake in her mouth, Mrs. Malhotra's words whirled in her ears. She had vocalized Mira's secret dream. Mira had been thinking of striking out on her own for so long, and Mrs. Malhotra was giving her the opportunity to take the leap.

The question was, did Mira have the courage to do so?

"How is it?" Mrs. Malhotra asked, leaning forward, breaking Mira's thoughts.

"Like sin!" Mira replied, chuckling at Mrs. Malhotra's satisfied smile.

"It is one of my favourite recipes," Mrs. Malhotra replied, settling back in her chair, her eyes beaming with pride. "Most of the recipes in the cafe are my own. I think that's why people call the food here comfort food."

"Stop!" Mira said with a laugh. "You are tempting me to take your offer. I will let you know after I return from the holiday, ok!"

Mrs. Malhotra's eyes twinkled. "Deal!" she said. "Now tell me, where are you going on holiday? Dev was also telling me something about it."

Mira couldn't control the guilt rising in her heart at the mention of Dev's name. She wondered if Dev had told his grandmother that he had asked her out and that Mira had refused.

Probably not, else why would she be so nice and welcoming? Mira thought, stalling by taking another bite of the cake.

Before Mira could reply, a voice spoke, "Hello, Grandma!"

"Dev!" Mrs. Malhotra cried in pleasure, as Dev leaned down to hug her. "This is a welcome surprise! You, dropping in on a working day."

Dev gave her a mischievous grin. "I was missing my favourite girl," he said.

Glancing at Mira, he gave her a quick nod.

Mira nodded back before looking down at the cake. She felt a little uneasy about seeing Dev. She had not expected to see him here. Judging by the smiles wreathing Mrs. Malhotra's face, neither had she.

Looking at the slice of carrot cake on Mira's plate, Dev said, "Looks like Grandma is bribing you for something. The famous carrot cake comes out only when she wants to bribe someone."

Mira's eyes flew to Dev's. Her worry that her refusal would affect their interactions evaporated upon seeing his friendly expression. She gave him a bright smile as Mrs. Malhotra gasped in mock outrage.

"Pish-posh! What a naughty boy you are to be revealing my secrets," scolded Mrs. Malhotra, swatting Dev's arm. "Mira was about to tell me about her holiday when you interrupted," she added.

Two pairs of eyes turned towards Mira, forcing her to reply. "Not a fancy holiday, just going for a relaunch of a cafe that a friend owns."

"What a coincidence! We are sitting in a cafe, talking about a relaunch. Are you arranging the party there as well?" Mrs. Malhotra asked.

Mira shook her head, her thoughts turning towards the unknown Sunita, who Mira was sure would hog the limelight. Pushing the thought away, she said, "No, I am just going to enjoy the party as a guest."

Mrs. Malhotra opened her mouth to ask more questions, but Mira's phone beeped, interrupting their conversation. Glancing at the screen, Mira said, "I am sorry. It is a meeting reminder. I need to leave."

"Sure, my dear, and do give a thought to my proposal," Mrs. Malhotra said, giving Mira a warm hug.

Giving Dev a cheery wave, Mira walked down the stairs into the street, thinking about Mrs. Malhotra's smiles and how they made one feel full of hope.

"Sit, I am getting a crick in the neck looking at you," Mrs. Malhotra said to Dev, whose eyes were following Mira as she walked out.

"Nice girl," Mrs. Malhotra said.

"Mmm," mumbled Dev absent-mindedly, taking the chair across from her.

"Interested?"

Dev gave a rueful grin. "I asked her out last night, but she turned me down."

"Oh, meeting her would have been upsetting for both of you!" Mrs. Malhotra exclaimed. "If I had known, I wouldn't have called her."

"Chill Grandma!" Dev said. "I asked her out, and she refused. I am not in love with her or anything. Though, I would like to be her friend."

Mrs. Malhotra patted his hand gently. "You are such a decent human. I feel proud you are my grandson."

"Considering you are the one who raised me, almost single-handedly, then I think you deserve a pat on your back too!" Dev replied with a cheeky grin.

Mrs. Malhotra laughed. "Flatterer!" she said, as cups of coffee were placed in front of them.

Mrs. Malhotra waited until they were alone before her tone became serious. "What really brings you here?" she asked.

Dev slipped a folder across the table towards her. "I received another letter today. He is asking for more money."

Mrs. Malhotra's eyes hardened. "He must have read about your product launch in the newspapers."

"How do you want me to handle it?" Dev asked.

Mrs. Malhotra sighed, looking around the cafe she had built with blood, sweat, and tears.

"I am tired of giving in to him and his demands. He is a leech who will not leave until he has sucked us dry. But now, no more. We fight back!" Mrs. Malhotra's voice was low but firm.

If Mira had been there, the hardness in Dev's smile would have surprised her. It was more a baring of teeth than a smile. "Atta girl! We will show him his place. We will need to go to the farmhouse."

"Why?" asked Mrs. Malhotra. "Can't your lawyers file a case against him?"

Dev nodded, "Yes, they will, but as owners, we will need to be there in court and show proof to the judges. We will need to stay there for some time, at least until the first hearing."

Mrs. Malhotra slumped in her seat. She didn't want to but knew Dev was right. The house belonged to her, and she needed to stake a claim on it.

Dev leaned forward, taking Mrs. Malhotra's hands in his warm grasp. "I know you don't like going there, but if you want to fight him, this is the only way."

"Very well," she said, sitting up straight, her voice coated in steel. "We will leave in ten days."

XIV

Come to me in the silence of the night;
Come in the speaking silence of a dream.

People milled around the sidewalk in front of the café, waiting, as the sedan came to a stop. From inside the car, Mira's eyes took in the changes made to the coffeehouse's exterior.

The old weather-beaten signboard on top had changed to an acrylic one hung over the door from a wrought iron frame. *Cafe Sunshine*, it proudly proclaimed, swaying in the gentle breeze.

Written in black on a daisy-yellow background, the effect was striking yet welcoming.

The gleaming glass of the window reflected the afternoon sun, spreading diamonds in the air. A thin red ribbon barred the light green door, waiting for Raghunath to cut it and formally announce the launch of the revamped coffeehouse as Cafe Sunshine.

Mira unlocked the car door, her eyes searching for only one person. When Mira told Raghunath that she was booking the same homestay for the holiday where she had stayed last time, Raghunath had not been pleased.

"How can you stay in a homestay when you have your own home?" he had argued.

"I don't want to impose," Mira had replied.

"Impose!" his voice betrayed the hurt he felt. "You are a friend. Friends don't impose. They demand," he had retorted.

"But Manan might think otherwise," Mira had objected.

"It is my house. Manan can go stay at the homestay if he objects."

Raghunath's tone had been final, making it clear to Mira that it was futile to argue with him anymore.

When she replayed the argument to Manan, he had laughed.

"You always overthink. *Dadu* is right. You have a home here. Why do you want to stay somewhere else? If you have extra money, you can pay me the same rate as the homestay. God knows, with all my money going into the renovations, I could do with some cash," he had teased.

Mira chuckled at his words but had been secretly elated. A month with Manan, living in his house!

However, they had barely talked to each other since Mira had reached last evening. Even today, he had left early in the morning to sort out last-minute glitches, leaving Mira to come with Raghunath.

Her eyes finally spotted him, his back to her, talking to a young woman. As if sensing her scrutiny, he turned. Their gazes clashed and held. For a few moments, the crowds, the relaunch, everything faded before the young woman placed a hand on his sleeve, once again claiming his attention.

Mira narrowed her eyes, taking in the familiar way Manan bent his head as the girl whispered in his ear.

Must be that paragon of virtue, Sunita, Mira thought, as a cough reminded her of her duties. Turning back, she helped Raghunath out of the car.

"Looks good, doesn't it?" Raghunath said, leaning on the cane.

Mira nodded, giving him a warm smile.

It had been a shock to her when she met Raghunath last night. She couldn't help but curse the swift march of time. She had just found Raghunath, who felt like family to her, but within a few months, he was looking frailer. While the last time he had been going on his regular walks, he now preferred to use a cane to steady himself. His frequency of walks too had reduced, according to Manan.

Lightly touching his elbow to steady him, she said, "Shall we, Uncle?"

Together they walked towards the door, where Manan waited. The young woman stood next to him, holding a decorated tray in her hands.

Raghunath beamed at the young woman, patting her gently on her shoulder. "Mira, this is dear Sunita. She is the one who convinced me to agree to the renovation. Most of the ideas you will see inside are hers."

The green-eyed monster in her bosom raised its head, on hearing the warmth and affection in Raghunath's voice. Somehow, Mira had started feeling very proprietary towards him. Mira gave a polite smile to Sunita, whose answering smile was considerably warmer.

"So glad to meet you, Mira. Raghu Uncle talks so much about you! Manan too!" Sunita gushed.

Did she add Manan's name to warn me he is off-limits? Mira thought, her eyes sharpening, but before Mira could reply, Manan spoke, "*Dadu?*" gesturing to the scissors on the tray in Sunita's hands.

Grinning, Raghunath picked up the scissors, and with a theatrical flourish, cut the ribbon as the bystanders applauded and hooted. No one could miss the pride in Raghunath's eyes as he patted Manan's back before stepping inside the cafe.

******

Mira's eyes took in the freshly painted walls, a darker green than the one on the door. The aroma of freshly baked bread had replaced the underlying slightly musty smell that had permeated the cafe earlier. New rattan chairs complimented the older, darker tables that were from the old coffeehouse. The exposed electrical wiring had been retained, though the light fixtures were new. Checking out a spoon with brass accents that glistened under the modern chandelier, Mira let out an annoyed huff.

Sunita and Manan had done an excellent job. The coffeehouse still retained its old-world charm but with a contemporary twist. Each detail, down to the indie music playing in the background, had been well-thought. With astute social media marketing, Mira could see Cafe Sunshine becoming a hit with tourists and locals.

"Hey!" Manan said, handing her a cup of coffee.

"Hey back!" Mira replied, her eyes softening at him looking handsome in a navy blazer and dark jeans.

"Looking good," he drawled, his eyes scanning her outfit.

Mira felt an irrational bolt of pleasure go through her spine at the appreciative gleam in his eyes. She was glad she splurged on a new summery yellow linen saree for the cafe's relaunch. It made her feel feminine and desirable. Even though she knew a person was more than the clothes they wore, thinking that she looked good gave her the confidence to face Sunita's casual elegance of a purple jumpsuit and heels.

"Matches with the signboard," she commented trying to act nonchalant. As if compliments from Manan were an everyday occurrence.

"Sure does," Manan agreed.

They smiled at each other before looking away. They stood side by side, in silence, watching the guests murmur appreciatively at the changes.

It was easier to chat on the phone, Mira thought, sneaking a peek at Manan, who was smiling at the guests but made no move to leave her side.

He finally made the first move.

"So, what do you think? How does it look?" Manan asked, gesturing to the room.

"I think it looks great," she replied

"Admit it, you weren't convinced about the renovation," he teased.

She smiled. "No, I wasn't. But I was wrong."

Manan whooped with laughter. "Ladies and gentlemen, mark this day! Mira Rajput finally admitted she was wrong!" He announced to the room.

Conscious of the curious looks thrown their way, Mira tucked a strand of her hair behind her ear.

"Hush now! Stop laughing!" she insisted. A smile tugged her lips, as Manan continued to chuckle. "I never said I am a know-it-all."

"No, but I do remember your outrage when I told you about the renovation," he replied, a teasing gleam in his eye.

Mira's smile faded as she remembered that ill-fated dinner. She looked towards Raghunath, who was talking to Sunita, her hands gesturing animatedly.

"Yes, but I do wish that Uncle's story had a closure."

"His story had a closure," Manan retorted. "Janaki left him. He should have moved on. At least now, after so many years, he is."

Mira sighed hearing the bitterness in Manan's voice against Janaki. How could she make Manan understand that Janaki's actions were selfless?

"What are you guys talking about?" Sunita asked, coming towards them, a smile on her lips.

"Mira was just saying how good the cafe looks," Manan replied, his tone not betraying that they had been on the verge of arguing a few moments ago.

"Yes!" Mira replied, giving her first honest smile to Sunita. "When Manan first told me about the renovation, I thought the coffeehouse would become a generic steel and chrome cafe, but I am glad its quaint charm is still there."

"No thanks to Manan," Sunita replied, her eyes rolling. "If he had his way, he would have gutted this place, plus he has atrocious colour sense. Can you believe he wanted to paint the walls pink? The fights we had!"

"Fights that I, quite obviously, lost!" Manan commented, waving his hand around the room.

Seeing the comfort and familiarity between Sunita and Manan, Mira started feeling like a third wheel. Excusing herself on the pretext of Raghunath beckoning her, she left them talking.

*****

"Sitting at the corner table again?" Mira asked, sliding into the chair across from Raghunath. He was seated alone at a table by the corner.

Raghunath gave a sheepish smile in reply. "Used to this corner," he replied.

"Still waiting for your friend?"

Raghunath shrugged his shoulders at Mira's question. "Sometimes, the reality is different from our desires. My heart has waited for a long time, but my brain knows it is time to move on. Anyway, how many years do I have left? I think I would rather spend them reading in my armchair than waiting on a hard chair in a cafe." He gave an exaggerated wriggle on the chair to emphasise his point.

But instead of the smile he expected, Mira placed her hand over his wrinkled ones. "One can always hope, no?" she said, her voice soft.

Raghunath nodded, and they both fell silent, content to look at the people enjoying the party.

From across the room, Manan observed Mira and Raghunath sitting quietly, their hands clasped across the table. He felt contentment settle in his heart.

Initially, when Raghunath became attached to Mira, Manan felt uncomfortable. He thought Mira's friendship would be transient, leaving Raghunath feeling bruised. Mira's not calling Raghunath after going back validated his doubts. But after that disastrous dinner, Mira had proved him wrong. Now, he could see the affection she had for Raghunath, and vice versa.

He looked at them with a small smile until Sunita claimed his attention again.

XV

ॐ

You did not come,
And marching time drew on, and wore me numb.

ॐ

The aroma of phlox and petunias mingled, teasing the senses. Hidden in the trees, birds chirped, and butterflies flitted around, sipping nectar from rainbow-hued flowers. The sounds were a far cry from the rumble of traffic Mira was used to. The soft winter sun warmed her toes as she wiggled deeper into the mat she had spread on the grass. The book she was planning to read lay forgotten on the side. Raghunath sat nearby on a lawn chair, engrossed in a newspaper.

"I am going to the cafe. Do you want to come?" Manan asked, popping his head out the kitchen window, jerking Mira out of her drowsiness.

Mira shook her head. She would have loved to spend time with Manan but knew he would be busy with work. For the moment, she was content to let the sun warm her toes and listen to the birds.

"*Dadu?*"

Raghunath, too, shook his head, surprising Mira.

Drowsiness forgotten, Mira sat up, hugging her knees. She waited until she heard the engine of Manan's car fading before asking, "Have you given up on Janaki?"

Raghunath looked up from the newspaper, his eyebrows raised.

"Who told you about Janaki?" he asked.

Mira looked a little shamefaced, before replying, "Manan."

"It was not his secret to tell," Raghunath replied, uncharacteristically stern.

Mira got up from the mat to crouch next to Raghunath's chair.

"Please don't be angry. I was the one who forced him. He didn't mean to betray your confidence. He cares about you a lot."

Folding the newspaper, Raghunath said, "I cannot be angry at that boy. I love him a lot. And no one can 'force' the boy to do anything he doesn't want to." Raghunath patted Mira's hand and sighed, "It is ok that you know."

"Why are you not going to the cafe? Have you given up hope?" Mira probed, unable to give up on the idea of Raghunath not waiting for Janaki.

Raghunath looked towards the flower beds with eyes that were hazy with memories. "What purpose will be solved? At least now, one table will be free for the paying customers," Raghunath added dryly.

"Do you still love her?"

"I have loved her for almost my whole life. Now I know nothing else," he replied.

"Then don't give up! Find her, make her acknowledge your love!" Mira cried.

Raghunath shook his head, his wrinkles deepening. "Dear *beta ji*, I know you want my love story to have a happy ending. But all love stories reach that happy stage only by a stroke of luck. For most of us, love shrivels and atrophies. My love sustained me, giving me hope for so many years. But now my spirit and body grow weary. I want to live the rest of my life in peace and not look up whenever the doorbell tinkles."

The pain in his eyes broke Mira's heart. Unable to control herself, Mira reached out to hug Raghunath.

"Shall I make a cup of tea for you?" Mira asked, wiping her tears after a few minutes.

"Tea would be good," Raghunath replied, trying to get out of the chair.

Pressing his shoulder with a gentle hand, Mira said, "Enjoy the sun. I will bring it."

The conversation with Raghunath played in Mira's mind as she went through the motions of making tea. Raghunath might say he had given up on Janaki, yet Mira's gut said that without Janaki, Raghunath wouldn't find peace.

The question was how to find her.

The honk of a car's horn broke Mira's musings. Turning off the gas, she poured the tea into two cups and walked into the garden. She was surprised to see Sunita seated on the grass next to Raghunath's chair, laughing and chatting.

Seeing Raghunath tweak Sunita's ear mockingly and her giving an exaggerated yelp, Mira felt her eyes prick. The affection between Raghunath and Sunita couldn't be faked. It had come from years of familiarity, and of having deep roots.

When Mira had lost her parents, she had not only lost her family; She had lost her sense of belonging. Mira realized that more than jealousy, Sunita aroused a longing in her heart. A longing for roots, which Mira wanted in this town.

Spotting her standing on the side, tea tray in hand, Raghunath exclaimed, "Come *beta ji*. Listen to the tall tales Sunita is telling!"

Pasting a smile on her face, Mira walked forward.

"Raghu Uncle, are you saying that town gossip is a tall tale?" Sunita replied, placing a hand over her heart in mock outrage.

Turning to Mira, she added, "I came to meet you. It was so crowded at the cafe yesterday that there was hardly any opportunity to talk. I have heard so much about you from Uncle and Manan that I would like to know you better."

Sunita's warm smile forced Mira to reciprocate. "Likewise. They talk very fondly of you. They told me how much you helped during the renovation."

"Manan told me he was headed to the cafe in the morning. I thought I would show you the town and we can get to know each other better?" Sunita asked, gesturing to the compact car parked on the side of the road.

Mira looked towards Raghunath. She wanted to spend some time with him, but this was a golden opportunity to probe not only about Sunita's feelings towards Manan but also if Sunita knew anything about Janaki. Being a local, Sunita would have the contacts Mira could tap into her search for Janaki.

Sensing her hesitation, Raghunath said, "Go explore the town, *beta ji*. The sun is making me drowsy. My poor, creaking bones need a nap. I will see you at dinner."

Mira gave him a quick smile and a hug. Turning to Sunita, she said, "Guess we are going for a ride."

XVI

Though I do my best I shall scarce succeed.
But what if I fail of my purpose here?

It had been ten minutes since Mira had waved Raghunath goodbye.

For the first few minutes, Mira had to remind herself to breathe. The roads were so narrow every time a car approached from the opposite side Mira's nerves would shoot up. She would brace herself for a head-on collision before the cars would pass by with a whisker of space between them. It took her some time to realise that even though the roads were narrow, Sunita was a pro in hill driving, expertly maneuvering the car through the twisted mountain road.

Once Mira was sure she could manage a conversation without hyper-ventilating, she decided it was time to probe Sunita. "How do you know Uncle and Manan?" She asked.

Sunita changed the gears before replying. "Raghu Uncle was a close friend of my grandfather, and I was very close to my grandfather. Whenever grandfather visited Uncle, I would tag along. Thus, Manan also became my friend. We were practically inseparable while growing up. But then I was sent to the US for my studies. Even though some distance has cropped up, Manan is still one of my closest friends. My grandfather passed away a few years ago. Meeting Raghu Uncle makes me miss him a little less."

"So sorry about your loss," Mira said, lightly touching Sunita's arm with her fingertips.

Sunita shrugged. "That's life, no? Death has to be faced. It makes one realise how little time we have on Earth. That's why I make sure that I always stay in touch with Raghu Uncle and Manan. They are too precious." She added, glancing at Mira with a soft smile.

Mira's heart softened seeing the hidden pain in Sunita's eyes. No one knew the pain of the loss of family better than her.

The warmth in Sunita's voice, when she talked about Manan and Raghu, showed that she was genuinely fond of them. But did her caring for Manan go deeper into love? That was not clear. But she couldn't ask this question outright. Not liking the flare of jealousy against Sunita, even though the poor girl had not done anything wrong until now, Mira decided to change the direction of the conversation to ask about Janaki.

"To tell you the truth, I was surprised when Manan told me about the coffeehouse's transformation," Mira confessed.

"Why?"

"When Manan told me Raghunath Uncle and Janaki's love story, I never thought Uncle would give up waiting for Janaki."

"Manan told you the story!" Sunita exclaimed. "Manan never tells it to anyone. Ever! He didn't tell me, despite me bugging him for years! I know the story only because my grandfather told it to me."

Mira felt her heart pop with joy at learning that Manan had not revealed Janaki's story to Sunita. The fact Manan trusted her enough to share a piece of his family's history, made her feel that maybe Manan was not unaffected by her.

Trying to keep her voice casual, she asked, "Why do you think Uncle agreed to the renovation?"

Sunita shook her head. "Honestly? I don't know. A few years ago, when Manan bought the coffeehouse, he had asked for permission to renovate it. Uncle told him a strict no. The coffeehouse would never be renovated while he was alive, he had declared. Manan and Uncle had had a big fight, but ultimately Manan had given in. A few months ago, just to poke the bear, I casually told Raghu Uncle the coffeehouse was looking a little run down. Hearing my words, he decided it would be renovated. His decision was so unexpected that it took everyone by surprise. Including Manan."

"Do you think he has given up on Janaki?" Mira asked hesitantly.

Sunita shrugged.

"Maybe," she replied. "But you know, once in a while, I still see his eyes glued to the cafe door, as if he is waiting for her to walk in. Plus, he did insist that the bell be put on the door."

"But why are you asking about Raghu Uncle and Janaki?" Sunita asked, taking another bend, as the car climbed higher up the mountain road.

Keeping her eyes on the twisted mountain road, Mira decided to be honest. "Somewhere in my heart, I don't think

Uncle is over Janaki. I feel he will not find any peace or closure until he finds Janaki. I don't know why, but I trust Janaki. I believe she truly loved Uncle," Mira replied.

"You seem to be a romantic," Sunita said.

"This is the second time, I have been called romantic by a person from your town," Mira said chuckling wryly. "But don't you believe in Janaki and Raghunath Uncle's love?"

"What is love? In my family, there are only business transactions in the name of marriages that leads to the creation of babies," Sunita countered.

"Surely you believe that the emotion called love exists," Mira persisted, surprised to hear cynicism in Sunita's answer.

"Maybe," Sunita replied, noncommittal. "But why are you asking if I believe in love?"

Mira thought for a few minutes, wondering if she should confide in Sunita, before deciding to take the leap. "I want to look for Janaki. And I want your help," she blurted.

Sunita slammed the brakes, bringing the car to a sudden stop in the middle of the road.

"Sunita!" she shouted. At the same time, Sunita demanded, "Search for Janaki? Are you crazy?"

"Why? What's so crazy about searching for Janaki?" Mira asked, pulling on the seatbelt that had jerked her back. She nervously looked at the road. Sunita had stopped the car in the middle of a turn. A car could come and hit them. "Can you drive, you have stopped the car in the middle of the road!" she pointed out.

Ignoring Mira's point about moving the car, Sunita replied, "Well, for one, you do not have a single clue about Janaki. Not how she looked or where to start looking. Not to mention you would be meddling in Raghu Uncle's life."

"I am not meddling. I am just trying to get closure for Raghunath Uncle," Mira replied a little sullenly, her eyes still on the road.

"And what about Manan?"

"What about him?" Mira huffed, looking at Sunita.

"You do know he will hit the roof if he finds out that you are searching for Janaki? He detests Janaki and the toll her wait has taken on Uncle. Do you want to risk your friendship for someone who might not even be alive?" Sunita reasoned.

Mira looked back at the empty road curving ahead. Her voice was calmer as she replied, "You are correct. Manan is happy that Uncle has moved on from Janaki. But my heart knows I need to do this. I will keep my search for Janaki a secret."

"Secrets have a way of revealing themselves," Sunita warned.

"I will have to take the risk," Mira replied.

Sunita shook her head. "You are crazy to be doing this."

"You are repeating yourself. I know I am crazy for doing this. Just tell me if you will help me or not. And for heaven's sake, move the car!"

Finally, putting the car into gear, Sunita shrugged her shoulders. "Your craziness must have rubbed off on me. Let us go home and plot our strategy in searching for Raghu Uncle's Janaki."

Mira looked out of the car window as the car moved again. There was a small grin on her face.

XVII

On cloud, or land or mist or sea-
Love's solid land is everywhere!

"You have a beautiful home," Mira said as Sunita's car purred up the gravel drive towards a mansion a little beyond the town limits. Contrasting with the verdant forest surrounding it, the house gleamed like a pearl.

"It is a house with a roof and four walls," Sunita replied. "I prefer the warmth of Raghu Uncle's house. This one," she said, parking the car under the porch, "is just full of things collected to impress others."

Mira glanced at Sunita as she followed her through a foyer into an opulent living room. This was the second time Sunita had alluded to not having a happy home. There was something so sad about Sunita as she talked about love being materialistic that Mira wanted to probe more. But she stopped herself before she could ask anything intrusive. She didn't know Sunita that well. Their acquaintance had yet to blossom into friendship.

Gesturing to Mira to take a seat on one of the leather sofas that ringed the room, Sunita flopped on an armchair and asked, "Where shall we start?"

"Well, we know Janaki studied in the local college around the same time as Raghunath Uncle," replied Mira.

"And like him, she was also in the English Department," Sunita added. "Do you know her last name?"

Mira shook her head. "Manan mentioned it once, but I do not recall it now."

Sunita tapped her fingers on her phone. "If we knew her last name, we could check at the town hall, unless…"

"Unless?"

"Unless the college has records."

Unlocking her phone, Sunita scrolled through her contacts. Finding the one she was looking for she dialled a number. "I think the college digitised its records a few years back. Let me check if they have any Janaki in the records," she said, tapping her foot, waiting for the call to connect.

"Yes, hello! Is this Ms. Shailja? My name is Sunita, Mr. Kailash Sharma's daughter. I wanted to know how one can check the records of students in college. I want records of a student who studied in the sixties."

Mira moved to a sofa closer to Sunita as garbled nonsense from the headset reached her.

Sunita spoke again, "Hmm, ok. No, I need it for some research I am doing. Thank you!"

"Can we check the records?" Mira asked the minute Sunita disconnected the call.

"No," replied Sunita, "The lady says it is a breach of privacy."

Deflated, Mira slumped on the cushions. "Now what?"

"Now, we flex our clout. We go to her boss, the principal of the college, my father's golf buddy. He will get us an appointment to look at the records," Sunita replied with an impish grin.

Mira picked up her bag and stood up. Seeing Sunita still lolling in the armchair, Mira raised an eyebrow.

Sunita grinned at Mira's irritation. "The college timings are from eight to 4. It will be closed by the time we reach it. We should go tomorrow."

Deflated, Mira sank back into the couch.

"Would you like to have some tea? We can go back to Raghu Uncle's home later," Sunita said, getting up from the armchair.

"Sunita!" a soft, cultured voice spoke from the door of the living room. A woman, wearing a form-fitting shalwar-kameez, gauzy chiffon dupatta trailing on one shoulder, floated into the room. It was difficult to place how old the woman was. Her skin was smooth and un-lined, which was usually the effect of a few anti-ageing surgeries and expertly applied make-up.

Sunita, Mira noticed, immediately changed the moment the woman came. The customary mischief dancing in her eyes was missing. Instead, there was a smirk on Sunita's face as if she was deliberately trying to provoke the other woman.

"Sunita, why is that rust bucket you call a car standing under the porch instead of the garage? I cannot stop you from driving that thing, but I have told you not to park it in front many times. So many important people visit our home. What will they think? That Sharma's can't afford luxury cars?" The woman's tone was low but chiding.

"That so-called rust bucket is the car Grandpa got me for my 18th birthday. I had gone to meet Raghu Uncle and was showing my friend Mira around the town. I thought I would treat her to our cook's famous sandwiches. But now I think I will go to Cafe Sunshine," Sunita replied, picking up the car keys she had thrown on the coffee table earlier.

The woman glanced at Mira. Her eyes under dramatically long lashes, scrutinised Mira from head to toe. Finding Mira's casual attire and no make-up look, not worthy of even a quick hello, the woman turned back towards Sunita. This time, even though her facial expression didn't change, there was a hint of impatience in her tone. "I thought your father said he didn't want you to go to that ramshackle coffeehouse?"

Sunita's chin jutted out. Instead of replying, she turned to Mira and said, "Let's go!"

Mira hastily got up, eager to escape the drama in which she had involuntarily gotten caught when the woman spoke again.

"There is a delegation coming in half an hour. Your father wants you to make them comfortable until he comes. He is running a little late." The woman's message was clear.

Sunita's shoulders slumped a little.

"It is ok," Mira found herself saying. "I can go back myself."

"No, I will send you with a driver," Sunita said. Arching a brow at the woman, she added, "I do have some rights in the house. Isn't it, Mother?"

The woman looked away.

*****

Sunita tapped her fingers on the steering wheel in time with the music as she waited. It was still quite early in the morning. The sun had yet to dissipate the mist that swirled in tendrils around the trees. Ten minutes later, there was a knock on the window. Smiling, she unlocked the car for

Mira.

"What happened?" she asked, looking at Mira's guilty expression. "Why did you ask me to meet you at this turning? I could have picked you up from the house."

"Uncle asked me to go to the library with him. I fibbed, saying I wanted to explore the town alone today. So, I couldn't risk him finding out that I am going with you. I hate sneaking behind his back," Mira replied, buckling her seatbelt.

Sunita gave a sympathetic pat on Mira's shoulder. "I can understand. You are an honest person who wants everything aboveboard. But it is best to keep our quest a secret until we get a more solid lead."

She nodded as Sunita's car navigated the narrow lanes of the town. Mira hesitated a little before plunging in on the other thought troubling her. The whole night, she couldn't believe that the polished woman she had met in Sunita's home was her mother. They were as different as night and day. "About last evening..."

Sunita's lips twisted in a grimace. "Yeah, I am sorry you had to experience the special mother-daughter conversation."

Mira's heart ached at hearing Sunita's words. Her aversion to love made more sense after their interaction. Sunita and her mother had a distance between them that made Mira long for a hug from her mother. She decided to probe a little more.

"Your parents don't like you visiting Raghunath Uncle?"

"They don't like anything that doesn't bring monetary gain," came the reply. Before Mira could comment on her answer, she announced, "We are here."

Sunita parked in front of an imposing brick building. She laughed at Mira's awed expression. "What if the degree of our small-town college is not in demand anymore? At one time, this was the only college in the neighbouring five districts," she chuckled.

The bitterness of the altercation between Sunita and her mother receded as Mira followed Sunita towards the pillared portico into the college. They walked through the corridors as Sunita pointed out different rooms, but Mira's steps slowed as they reached the library.

Turning to Sunita, she said, "Do you mind talking to the Principal by yourself? He is your family friend, and I think it would be an imposition if I were also there. I want to have a look at the library."

Sunita raised a brow at Mira's words, but did not press the point. Giving her a short nod, Sunita purposefully strode down the corridor, her heels tapping on the stone floor while Mira pushed open the door to the library.

Mira felt as if she had stepped back in time. Racks upon racks of books towered over her. A little dark, the air was a mix of musty and magic.

Her feet took her towards the alcove tables flanking a wall. All of them were empty. The students had other things to occupy their time with. She skimmed her hand over the warm wood, looking at the scratches on the tables. There were initials intertwined with hearts or just single ones.

Maybe, for a moment, someone wanted to claim something for themselves, she thought, her fingertips lightly tracing the scratches.

Looking around, she wondered which table was Janaki's favourite.

"Mira?" a voice interrupted her thoughts. She turned to see Manan standing there, frowning.

Her heart gave a guilty start. She had assumed Manan would be at the cafe.

"What are you doing here?" he asked.

"I saw the college building while I was exploring the town. It looked so imposing that I wanted to check it out," she replied. She could feel her neck becoming warm as the lies tripped over her tongue.

Trying to overcome her confusion on seeing him unexpectedly, she asked, "What about you? Why are you here?"

Pointing towards the books in his hands, he said, "*Dadu* was planning to come with you to show you around, but when you said you wanted to be alone, he asked me to return them."

Mira flushed. Trying to quash her guilt, she said, "I didn't know Uncle meant this library."

"What other library would he mean in this small town?" he asked, his tone questioning her sanity.

Before Mira could defend herself, Sunita walked into the library grinning, a stack of papers in her hand. Spotting Manan, she schooled her expression to non-committal, quickly stuffing the papers into her handbag.

"Hi!" she said.

Manan raised his brow. "Why are you here?"

Sunita opened her mouth to reply, but Mira beat her to it.

"I bumped into Sunita just as I entered the college. She had a meeting with the Principal. We thought we would go for a drive once she was free." Mira's words tripped over her tongue in haste.

Sunita obediently nodded to corroborate her words.

"What kind of meeting?" Manan asked, his eyes suspicious.

"Er...something to do about a charity event," Sunita improvised.

Manan's brows rose higher. "Why do I feel that the two of you are up to something?"

"What nonsense!" Sunita chirped. "I am just showing Mira around our lovely town. Come, let us show her the canteen too. I spent most of the time there whenever I came to the college," she giggled.

Linking her arm with Manan's, she dragged him along, turning once to wink at Mira. Mira trailed behind, partially relieved Manan wasn't aware of their mission and partly annoyed by how Sunita had linked her arm with Manan's.

There was something inherently honest and charming about her that made Mira think Sunita could become the person one depended upon in troubled times. She had started liking the gregarious girl. But her closeness with Manan had made Mira's jealousy flare up again.

Seriously Mira, get yourself together, she scolded herself as she fake-smiled and sipped her tea, trying to involve herself in the conversation.

XVIII

And a voice less loud, thro' its joys and fears,
Than the two hearts beating each to each!

"Good night, *beta ji*. I am off to bed," Raghunath called out.

Mira looked up from the book she was reading in surprise.

Usually, Manan returned from the cafe by seven, and the three would have dinner together. However, since the assistant manager of the cafe had taken ill, Manan stayed back to supervise the cleaning and locking it for the night. Taking advantage of the chilly night, Raghunath and Mira lit a fire in the living room and spent a cosy evening quietly reading.

Curled up on the couch, Mira had been so engrossed in her book that she didn't realise it was almost ten.

"Good night, Uncle," she replied. "I think I will read a few more pages before turning in."

Raghunath nodded, leaving Mira alone with her book.

It was past eleven when there was the snick of the main door lock. Footsteps sounded in the corridor before Manan walked into the room. He glanced at Mira, who half-smiled at him before her eyes turned to her book.

Taking off his jacket, he draped it over the armchair before moving closer to the fire to warm his hands.

"*Dadu* went to bed?" he asked, half-turning towards her.

Mira nodded, not looking up from her book. Silence once again descended upon the room. Mira assumed Manan would leave her alone, as it was late, and Raghunath was asleep.

They had barely talked to each other ever since she had been in town. Manan had been busy ironing out the kinks after the relaunch. An awkward silence hung between them whenever they were together. After six months of talking for hours on the phone, it seemed as if they couldn't communicate in person.

However, Manan surprised her as he flopped on the couch beside her. Leaning back to rest his head, he closed his eyes as a soft sigh escaped his lips.

Mira sat up straighter. Adjusting the blanket she had wrapped around her legs she sneaked a look. The lines around his mouth had deepened with the strain of the past few months. Mira had an urge to caress his forehead. To give him comfort from the burdens he carried. Her hand lifted but stopped herself. Letting her hand fall to rest in the space between them, she asked, "Rough day?"

"Hmm," he mumbled, not opening his eyes.

Assuming he wanted to be left alone, she turned back to her book.

However, the words that had engrossed her now seemed like black scratches on a page. Every fibre of her being seemed to be aware of Manan's nearness. His cologne, mixed with the fragrance of bread from the bakery, tickled her nose, tempting her to move closer to him.

They sat side by side in silence. He, with eyes closed, and her eyes fixed on her book, trying to ignore the warmth of his lean hands just a hairbreadth away. The only sound in the room was the clock ticking each minute.

It felt warm. Intimate.

Mira thought Manan had fallen asleep as his chest rose and fell rhythmically with each breath, but suddenly, he spoke.

"What were you and Sunita doing in the college?"

Mira shrugged, "Nothing. Sunita has been showing me the town."

"I have been neglecting you. I should have been the one to show you around," Manan murmured, touching her fingers lightly before resting his hand on hers.

Mira felt her breath catch. The warmth of his hand seemed to penetrate her entire core, setting it aflame.

"I know you are busy," she replied, trying to ignore the thrill in her heart at his touch.

"I will take the day off tomorrow. Let's have a picnic together. Away from the cafe, away from the town," he said, opening his eyes to look at her.

"I would like that," Mira replied, her voice soft.

He looked as if he wanted to say something. Instead, he shifted closer, leaning towards her. The pressure on her hand increased, burning her. She willed her fingers to stay still, revelling in his touch. His eyes were like molten chocolate, tempting her, their expression intense. Her body infinitesimally swayed towards him. She felt as if she was standing on a precipice about to fall.

A shuffle sounded in the corridor. They looked at each other for another moment before Manan squeezed Mira's hand and got up. He walked out of the room, leaving Mira sitting stunned on the sofa.

She heard Manan murmuring to Raghunath, who had gone to the kitchen for a glass of water, before walking him back to his room. The house grew quiet, yet she stayed seated on the couch, the warmth of Manan's touch lingering on her hand.

Were they about to kiss? Mira wondered as she waited for Manan to return, trying to interpret the expression she had seen in Manan's eyes. The fire died down, but Manan didn't return. Finally, the cold drove her to her bed.

XIX

Two lovers by a moss-grown spring:
They leaned soft cheeks together there.

Manan kept his promise of taking the day off.

"We will go for a picnic," he announced at breakfast the next morning.

Unsure, Mira looked at the toast on her plate, trying to stall.

Yes, Manan was her friend, but he was also the man whom she loved. After their brief interaction in the night, her feelings were too close to the surface. Except for touching her hand, a touch, that was seared into her memory, Manan had not given any indication or sign that he was interested in her romantically.

"But the cafe?" she asked.

"It can survive a day without me," came the calm reply.

"Raghunath Uncle?"

Mira glanced at Raghunath, who chuckled. "You think my bones will survive the rattling over the roads to reach a picnic spot deemed suitable enough by Manan? No, *beta ji!* You both go and have fun. I will enjoy the sun in the comfort of my garden and a long afternoon nap."

"So?" Manan asked.

Mira looked Manan, temptation warring with practicality in her heart.

"Yeah, ok," she mumbled, trying to quell tiny jolts of current coursing through her veins.

****

"Ready?" Manan asked.

Mira nodded as she buckled her seat belt. Waving Raghunath goodbye, she settled in the seat, keeping her eyes firmly on the road, trying to ignore the waft of Manan's cologne.

"I was thinking of playing Altaf Raja on the drive," Manan drawled twenty minutes later. The town had fallen behind as the car ventured deeper into the forests that surrounded the town.

"Seriously?" she asked, half-turning towards him, her eyebrows almost touching her hairline in surprise.

"He is quite popular," Manan commented.

"Yeah, with *autowallahs!*" Mira shot back.

"Are you saying they don't have feelings? What a snob!" His lips twitched as he waited for her reaction.

She looked at him sternly, her brows arched.

He barked out a short laugh. "Well, mentioning Altaf Raja did make you look away from the window and talk to me!"

Mira blushed. They had driven across the town in excruciating silence. Mira had mentally picked and discarded topics for conversation. She was unsure how to behave. As a casual friend, or something more? She compromised by keeping her attention on the scenery flying by the window, rather than noticing the way the tendons in Manan's forearms flexed whenever he changed the gears.

"No more talk of Altaf Raja! We will listen to Bollywood music from the nineties," she announced, picking up her phone.

Manan gave a theatrical groan. "Hindi music? Really?"

"Yes, Mr. Cafe Owner. I know you like soft melodies."

"*Dadu* likes those songs."

"But Uncle doesn't go to the cafe anymore, and you still play them."

"I didn't get the time to make a new playlist," he muttered.

Mira continued to look at him.

Giving in, Manan let out an impatient huff. "Fine! Play your Bollywood tunes! And make sure you add songs from Ashiqui.The old one!"

Mira let out a gurgle of laughter at his sheepish expression, and soon, the car was filled with Kumar Sanu's crooning.

As the day progressed, Mira's inhibitions fell away. She decided the future was too far. It was best to enjoy the precious moments she had with Manan alone.

After driving for more than an hour, Manan stopped by a secluded bank of trees. Taking out the picnic hamper from the boot, he held out his hand. Mira hesitated before keeping hers in it, delighting in the warmth of his clasp.

Manan smiled. One he had never given her before. Tender, full of unspoken promises.

Lacing his fingers with hers, he led her narrow path through the trees.

"What is this place?" Mira asked, curious, as she stepped carefully through the pebbled trail.

"A place that is very special to me. I used to come here often with my father," Manan replied.

Mira felt happiness burst in her upon hearing Manan's words. She was glad that he had brought her to a place that held special memories for him.

The path twisted and turned before coming to a clearing surrounded by pine trees. Mira gasped at seeing the beauty surrounding her.

"It seems right out of a fairy tale!" she cried, her eyes widening at the exquisite vista.

The sky was a spotless blue, with nary a cloud to mar its surface. It contrasted with the green of the meadow. Cutting through the meadow, a narrow stream flowed, gurgling over the river stones. On its banks was a riot of wildflowers, adding colour and joy.

"Only a small cottage is missing," she said, spreading her arms wide, giving a little twirl.

"Would you like a cottage here?" Manan asked.

Looking at him, Mira laughed. "Of course, I would. I would love to have a thatch-roofed cottage with smoke lazily rising from the chimney. The cottage would, of course, be full of books. A total cliché, but one that would fit perfectly in this setting."

"Well, my lady, since I can't build a cottage right now, will a picnic blanket do?" Manan teased, spreading a gaily printed blanket under a tree. He opened the picnic basket and started unpacking the food.

Mira pouted. "It is too early to eat. Let's go into the water first."

"The water is coming straight from the mountains. It is going to be too cold! Better to soak the sun, get some Vit-D that you city people lack," Manan replied, proceeding to sprawl on the blanket.

"No, you can't be practical today, Manan. You are on a holiday. You brought me here, and now you have to make sure I am happy," Mira argued, sitting on the blanket next to him to take off her sneakers. Rolling up the hem of her jeans, she stood up, looking at him expectantly.

Manan refused to budge and instead sprawled further. Shrugging, Mira skipped towards the stream. Manan turned to his side. Propping his head on his elbow, he watched her. This unexpected childish side of hers amused him.

"Ok, but be careful. Some of the stones might be too smooth. You might slip," he warned, from his position on the blanket.

Looking back, Mira stuck her tongue out at him. "Spoilsport," she taunted. Turning back, she took the first tentative step into the water. She gasped the moment the icy cold water hit her feet.

From the bank, she could hear laughter from Manan. She turned to glare at him. "Don't you dare say I told you!" She threatened.

He held out his hands, palms upwards in a gesture of innocence, though, even from the distance, Mira could see his lips twitch.

As her feet got used to the coldness, she walked further into the water, lifting her head to look around. She felt her senses come alive in this wonderland. Crystal-clear water shimmered like diamonds as the sunlight hit it. The warm sun on her back contrasted with the iciness of the water swirling around her toes. The zephyr caressing her skin made her feel lighter as if she could float away into the clouds.

She closed her eyes, concentrating on storing the sensations, the emotions aroused in her heart.

From the bank, Manan looked at her, enjoying the moment, and felt his breath catch at the picture she made. She looked like a fey, the *aacharis* the hill folk warned about. The mountain nymphs who ensnared the unsuspecting with their beauty. If he was not careful, she would possess him like the *aacharis*.

As if sensing his scrutiny, Mira turned. Looking straight at Manan, she smiled, but her smile faded as their eyes locked. As if he were a puppeteer pulling her towards him with an invisible thread, Mira started walking back towards the bank.

Not caring where she stepped, she had almost reached the bank when her foot slipped. She teetered trying to catch her balance but could feel her body fall. Closing her eyes tight, she braced for the impact with the icy water, when warm hands clutched her arms, pulling her to the bank.

She warily opened her eyes to see Manan looking down at her. His eyes burned with a fire she had not seen before. His hands did not leave her arms once she found her footing. Instead, they slipped down to her elbows. His touch was firm but tender, as if cradling her.

"I told you to be careful," he murmured.

Trapped by the emotion in his eyes, Mira could not answer.

His hand lifted to push away the strands of hair that had freed themselves from the ponytail behind her ear. His fingertips lingered, trailing down her cheek, leaving fire in their wake before finally resting on her jaw.

Her expression must have given away what her heart desired, for his head dipped down and he touched his lips to hers. Letting out the breath she had been holding, Mira's fingers fisted in his shirt, pulling him closer. It was all the signal Manan needed as he deepened the kiss.

Lost in his kiss, Mira did not realise when they moved to the blanket. The kisses grew wilder, deeper with whispered endearments. Instinctively, she arched towards him as he pressed her deeper into the blanket. She ran her hands over his muscular arms, down his toned torso. His touch, in return, left a trail of fire wherever he touched. Mira felt as if she had the whole world in her hands as she revelled in the strength of Manan surrounding her.

Moments, seconds, hours. Mira did not know how much time had lapsed as they lay together on the blanket under a blue sky. Snug in Manan's arms, Mira felt she was in a cocoon, isolated from the world and its problems.

All that mattered was here and now. She, in Manan's arms, her head on his chest, hearing his heart beating with a steady thump.

"Tell me about when you and your father would come here," Mira asked after the first rush of passion cooled. She was curious to know more about the man she had fallen in love with.

"My father was one of the gentlest people you could have met. He used to bring me here during holidays. We used to hike deeper into the woods, and he would tell me folk tales. Sometimes, Ma would also come with us. We would have a picnic then, with aloo-puri and halwa. He would sing funny songs, making Ma laugh," Manan said.

Mira could feel him smiling as he said this.

"He was always bringing home injured strays. Once, he found a dog. A car had crushed its leg. We tried to save it, but the injuries were too grievous. The dog died after a month. I was eight, and I remember crying and refusing to eat for almost a week. My parents argued after that incident. It was their first argument in front of me. Ma put her foot down after that. No more strays. The emotional cost was too much, she said."

Mira tightened her hands around Manan, feeling sad for the sensitive young boy he had been.

Manan caressed her head, his fingers lingering in the silky strands of her hair. "My mother's lessons used to be harsh, but she made me realise that one cannot survive in this world with one's head in clouds, like my father and *Dadu*."

"Why do you call Raghunath Uncle *Dadu*? You said there is a story there?" Mira asked.

"There is always a story. And you, my curious cat, want to know everyone's secrets," he replied.

Mira heard Manan's chest rumble as he chuckled. This Manan, she realised, was different from the Manan she had first met in the café. This Manan was softer. That Manan ignited a passion in her with his devotion to Raghunath. This Manan stripped away all her defences with his tender touch and teasing.

Manan picked up Mira's hand. Pressing a soft kiss on her palm, he started speaking again. "My story is not as romantic as *Dadu* and Janaki's. *Dadu's* original plan was to emigrate to the States after he completed his doctorate. But falling in love with Janaki changed them. His vow to wait for Janaki tied him to the town. He joined the college as a faculty.

"Frustrated by the constant pressure of his mother to get married, he moved out of his family's home. My father was the son of *Dadu's* caretaker. Fond of my father, *Dadu* made sure he got a decent education and job in the city. The salary was not much, but it was sufficient for us to have a decent life. We used to come back to the town for the holidays, where I would spend most of my time either with my father, tramping through these forests or with *Dadu*, listening to stories.

"One year during the holidays, Ma wanted to go to Kedarnath for a pilgrimage. Everything was ready, but two days before we were supposed to leave, I fractured my foot. My parents were in a quandary. The tickets were expensive. Cancelling them would mean money down the drain. Money that they had saved for months. But there was no way I could travel. Hearing their predicament, *Dadu* suggested to my parents that he would take care of me while they went on the pilgrimage.

"I was happy to hear *Dadu's* solution. Pilgrimage was not my idea of how one should spend the summer holidays. The day they waved me goodbye from the bus was the last time I saw them. A landslide, triggered by flash floods, swept them away. Their bodies were found downstream after a week. My grandfather, *Dadu's* caretaker, had already passed away a few years ago, and no one from my mother's family wanted another child to feed. Suddenly, at ten, I was an orphan with no family. *Dadu* formally adopted me, and we became each other's family."

Mira couldn't stop the tears from welling up in her eyes.

"Don't cry, dearest," Manan said, hearing her sniffle. Hugging her closer, he said, "I had *Dadu* with me, and he brought me up with love."

"Is that why you didn't leave the town like the other young people to go to the city? You felt you owe it to Uncle?"

Manan shook his head. "I did go to the city right after graduation. Even got a well-paying job there. But I couldn't live away from this small town. This place is not just in my bones, it is in my soul. So, I came back. Maybe it was destiny. A few months later the coffeehouse came on the market. The owner, a friend of *Dadu's*, was emigrating to Canada to live with his daughter. I decided to take the plunge and bought it."

"And there I met you, grumpy and condescending," Mira said, turning her face towards him.

"And there I met you, inquisitive and gorgeous," he replied, dropping a soft kiss on her lips.

*****

Mira and Manan were quiet on the drive back home. But this time, the silence was not uncomfortable. It was the silence of companionship.

Mira rolled down the window and inhaled, filling her lungs with the pristine chilly air perfumed with the fragrance of fresh grass and pine needles. The wind ruffled through her unbound hair. She had lost her scrunchie in the grass somewhere. She knew it would be painful later when she would have to brush out the tangles, but for now, she was content to lean her head out and let her thoughts wander as Manan drove through the mountain roads. Her emotions had been through a wringer, and her senses still tingled from Manan's kisses. She was conscious of the fact that Manan trusted her enough to share his story with her, but the guilt of going behind his back to find Janaki gnawed at her.

Mira knew that Manan would disapprove of her quest. Janaki had hurt Raghunath, which made her a villain in Manan's eyes.

Maybe I should confess..., Mira thought as they approached the house.

"Manan...," she started, getting out of the car when her mobile rang.

Frowning, she saw it was Sunita. Gesturing for Manan to continue ahead she took the call.

"Where are you?" Sunita asked without preamble. "I have been trying to call you since morning."

Mira looked at Manan, who was talking to Raghunath in the garden.

Loathe to share that she had spent the day with Manan, she replied, "I was exploring the forests. I guess there was no signal there."

"Is it?" Sunita replied. Her tone was dry, as if aware that Mira was hiding something.

"Why were you trying to reach me? Anything important?" Mira asked, trying to change the track of the conversation.

"I went through all the Janaki's in the college records and may have found the address of Raghu Uncle's Janaki. Do you want to check it out tomorrow?"

"Do you think the same family will be living there? I mean, it was a long time ago," Mira asked doubtfully.

"Worst case, it is a dead end. But what if we do find something there?" Sunita countered.

Sunita is right, Mira thought, walking towards Manan and Raghunath. *There is no harm in checking it out. And I will confess everything to Manan, depending upon the outcome of tomorrow.*

XX

And yet, by heaven, I think my love as rare
As any she belied with false compare.

Sunita and Mira stared at the massive black gate in front of them. High brick walls, covered with ivy, hid the house and its massive grounds from the views of the public. Set on the edge of the forest, a fair distance from the town centre, the property screamed old money.

"Seems like Janaki's family was loaded!" Sunita said, her voice awed.

"Do you know the family?" Mira asked, assuming they might be moving in the same social circle since Sunita belonged to the town's elite.

Sunita shook her head. "Never met them. I think my father visited the family once, but that was years ago. What

I know is that the family moved to the city years ago. They visit rarely, and that too only for short durations. They even bring their servants. Except for a couple of gardeners, who act as caretakers when the family is not in residence, no one lives here."

"It's pretty fancy for a home that is used occasionally. How do we know that the family is in town now?" Mira asked.

"The local grocer said someone ordered bread, eggs and milk yesterday from the mansion, so I assume someone is there or about to visit. Shall we?" Sunita asked, pointing towards the intercom button under the discrete brass nameplate that read Captain Ajay Malhotra.

Static crackled before a gruff voice asked, "*Haanji?*"

"We need to meet Mrs. Janaki," Sunita replied.

"No one of that name lives here."

"Can we meet someone from the family?"

"We have orders not to let anyone enter," the voice replied.

"Can you give us their phone number?" Mira asked.

"No," replied the voice before disconnecting.

Sunita and Mira looked at each other, stumped.

"Dead end," muttered Sunita, getting into the car and slamming the door.

Mira was silent as she buckled herself in.

Noticing her distraction, Sunita asked, "What happened?"

Mira shook her head. "Nothing. Just wondering if we are doing the right thing by searching for Janaki?"

"Weren't you the one who came to ask for my help in your search? Why the qualms now?" Sunita asked, incredulous.

"Manan..." Mira tried to search for words to explain what was in her heart. Searching for Janaki felt a lot like cheating on Manan. The side of Manan she had seen the day earlier had been too precious. She felt safe in his arms.

"You knew Manan would hit the roof if you searched for Janaki, but you still went ahead." Sunita's sharp words made Mira wince.

"But what if Uncle is hurt by our actions?" Mira

"Do you honestly think Raghu Uncle has moved on?" Sunita countered.

Mira thought of the times she had seen Raghunath staring into space, lost in memories when he thought no one was looking at him. She sighed. "I don't think Janaki will ever be out of Uncle's heart."

"Then we continue our search. Manan will come around once we find Janaki and Raghu Uncle is happy," Sunita replied, her voice ringing with conviction.

"But how?" Mira asked, gesturing towards the gate that remained obstinately shut. "The only lead is a dead end."

"We are smart girls. We will figure it out," Sunita replied, putting the car into drive. "Let us go to the cafe and decide what to do next. I am feeling peckish."

****

Manan frowned on seeing Mira and Sunita enter the cafe together.

"Why do I have the feeling that both of you are hatching a devious plot?" he said, guiding them towards an empty table.

"If we were hatching a plot, we wouldn't tell you, would we?" Sunita retorted.

"I could make you," he drawled, looking at Mira with such heat in his eyes that Mira blushed.

Noticing how Manan's eyes lingered on Mira, almost caressing and the rising red on Mira's cheeks, Sunita felt a pang in her heart. She had always been fond of Manan. She had hoped that one day, Manan would look at her with something more than friendship. But his interest seemed to have been captured by the pretty girl from the plains.

Clearing her throat theatrically, she gave a little push to Manan.

"Go get coffee and let us talk in peace," she grumbled.

Manan chuckled. Touching Mira's nose with a finger, which made her blush deepen, he sauntered back to the kitchen.

"Here!" Sunita said, snapping her fingers before Mira's glazed eyes as she followed Manan's retreating back. Mira gave a sheepish smile at Sunita's wry expression.

"Now I understand why you are suddenly hesitant in your search for Janaki. Love, is it?" Sunita asked.

"Head over heels," Mira replied, a little surprised she was sharing her innermost feelings with Sunita. "Is it okay with you that I'm in love with Manan?""

Sunita looked at her in surprise. "Why should I not be?"

Mira hesitated for a few seconds, choosing her words carefully. "I somehow felt that what you felt for Manan was more than friendship."

Sunita gave a small smile in reply. "You are very perceptive. Yes, I liked Manan and wished he could be more than a friend. But it is to you to whom he sent that smouldering gaze just now. I think Manan friend-zoned me a long time back."

"You are ok with it?"

Sunita shrugged. "My feelings are my concern. If Manan had been interested in me, I would have been happy. But all I am feeling right now is a twinge of disappointment. So, did

I love him? I think not."

Mira looked into Sunita's eyes and found nothing but honesty there.

Understanding her look, Sunita gave a rueful smile in return. "You know, I don't even know if love is for me."

"Why do you say that?" Mira asked. "What made your faith in love weak?"

"It is not that I do not believe in love. I believe in it. Raghu Uncle's love for Janaki is true. But that is the only example of steadfast love that I have seen. And that love story is also incomplete. In my family, matches are made to advance business prospects. My parents got married because of the land and paper mill that was part of her dowry. They tolerated each other for a year until I was born. Then they became indifferent. Both are addicted to changing lovers like clothes, oblivious to whom they hurt."

The bitterness in Sunita's tone told more about her to Mira than the past few days. Sunita's gregarious and cheerful personality hid a deep sadness in her heart.

Reaching out, she hugged Sunita. Startled by Mira's display of affection, Sunita laughed, "What is the hug for?"

Drawing back, Mira said, "You know, when I first heard your name, I was so jealous that Manan had such a good friend. But after spending these days with you and getting to know you, I realized you truly are the best friend one could have."

Sunita's answering smile was tinged with sadness. "That's what I am, the best friend in the whole world!" Slipping into a chair, she asked, "So, what's the plan? Will you leave your job and move here?"

Mira shook her head, sitting on the chair across from her. "Too soon to make plans. We have not even declared our love in words. But yes, my heart desires a future with

Manan."

Placing her hand on Mira's, Sunita said, "I am happy for both of you."

Mira smiled back. "Thank you! Anyway, let's move on from my love life and figure out what our next step should be."

Soon Sunita and Mira were engrossed in trying out ways to reach out to the people who lived in the mansion.

"Social media?" Sunita asked.

Mira nodded. "But how will we know which Janaki is the one we are looking for? Neither of us knows how she looks, nor do I think Uncle has any photograph of Janaki."

"Maybe we look at location tags on Instagram and see if someone has tagged that mansion?" Sunita suggested.

"How will we reach out?"

Before Sunita could reply, the bell on the cafe's door tinkled. Mira instinctively looked towards the door. She squealed in surprise at seeing the man who had entered.

"Dev!" she called out, jumping to her feet.

Dev turned at the sound of her voice, his face breaking into a big grin. Coming closer, he enveloped her in a hug.

"How come you are here?" Mira asked.

"Our family has a home here. Grandma had been feeling a little unwell for the past few weeks, so I thought a change of scene and good mountain air would help her get back on her feet. I saw the board of the cafe on the way. There was quite a buzz about it on social media. I decided to check it out and come for a coffee. But meeting you here was a bonus I had not counted on."

"I am so glad you are here," Mira said. Taking his hand, she pulled him towards their table. Gesturing to Sunita, she said, "This is my friend, Sunita. Come sit with us."

Dev nodded at Sunita, before taking the chair next to Mira.

"Where is Aunty?" Mira asked.

"Exhausted by the long drive, resting at home," Dev replied. "She anyway doesn't leave home whenever she is here. She says the home has everything she needs."

Just then, Manan walked up to their table.

"A friend?" he asked Mira, his eyes inscrutable.

"Yes, this is my friend, Dev Malhotra. Our company handled his product launch. The reason you had to re-schedule the dates for the cafe's relaunch," Mira replied, unable to keep her face from breaking out into a big grin.

As the men shook hands, Mira felt that silent communication was passing between them. Manan's expression was stern, his shoulders rigid. He looked aloof and condescending, just as he had when she had met him for the first time. Even Dev, who usually sported a good-humoured grin, looked serious.

She turned to Sunita to see if she also felt something weird between their interaction but saw her looking at Dev with a puzzled look.

Leaning forward, Sunita asked, "Where is your home, Dev?"

"It is on the furthest mountain road, just before the national forest."

Sunita turned to Mira; her eyes lit with excitement.

"Captain Ajay Malhotra!" she exclaimed, jumping up.

Dev frowned. "How do you know my father's name?"

It was now Mira's turn to stare at Dev. "Your father's name is Ajay Malhotra, and your home is the mansion at the farthest edge of town?"

Dev nodded, puzzled by why the two women were asking these questions.

Mira, too, jumped up. Clutching each other's arms, the two girls screamed, "We got the breakthrough!"

"What breakthrough are you talking about?" Manan asked, his voice cutting through their excitement like a whip.

Sunita and Mira stopped in their tracks. They stared at each other before Sunita gave an encouraging nod to Mira.

"Well, you see, we were trying to find Janaki. The last address in the college records was the same as Captain Malhotra's. We had gone in the morning, but the guard said no one was home. Now we hope Dev, or his grandmother, can help us find clues about Janaki," Mira said, pointing towards Dev, who still looked baffled.

"You mean to say that you were searching for Janaki, without telling me or *Dadu*?" Manan thundered, making Mira wince.

Mira tried to reason. "Manan, I just want Uncle to have closure."

"He has stopped coming here and waiting for her, hasn't he?" Manan retorted.

"He may have stopped coming to the cafe, but in the privacy of his heart, he still waits for her," Mira argued.

Manan leaned towards Mira, towering over her, his eyes shooting flames of anger. "Who gave you the right to meddle in our life?" he asked, his tone biting.

"Manan...," Sunita murmured, placing a hand on his sleeve, trying to deflect his anger.

Manan shrugged away Sunita's hand. His eyes bore into Mira's. "Please leave. You are no longer welcome here."

Spinning on his heel, Manan stomped back into the kitchen, leaving Mira shell-shocked by his words. Tears streamed down her cheeks as her heart splintered into a thousand pieces.

Sunita's arms came around her. Hugging Mira gently, she whispered, "Let's go."

Unresisting, Mira followed Sunita and Dev. At the cafe's door, she glanced back towards the kitchen door where Manan stood with his arms crossed, the lines of his body unyielding. Eyes that had once been full of love and warmth now glittered with anger.

Swallowing a sob, Mira shut the cafe door. The bell tinkled softly.

XXI

I told my love, I told my love,
I told her all my heart.

The sun was about to set when Sunita stopped the car at a little clearing. She looked at Mira's tear-swollen face and suppressed a sigh. If Manan had been in front of her, she would have given him a piece of her mind, and maybe a couple of kicks on his shins, too. He had always been a pig-headed fool who saw things only his way. He had failed to notice the depth of Mira's love for him and the fact that Mira was searching for Janaki because she deeply cared for Raghunath.

Patting Mira's shoulder, she said, "We will stop the search. Your relationship with Manan is more important. I am sure things will be back to normal in a few days."

Mira stared out the car window, watching the sky get darker, trying to control her tears. She had no recollection of getting into Sunita's car and for how long they drove through the mountain roads. Her heart felt as if a bulldozer had gone over it, leaving it flattened and bruised. How could Manan do this to her? Kicking her out of the cafe and not even try to listen and understand what she wanted to say.

Under the pain, a spark of anger ignited. Mira whispered, "No."

"Manan...," Sunita said, trying to convince Mira, but Mira shook her head

"No! I will not stop. I love Manan, but he cannot dictate and tell me what to do. I will find Janaki. I know Uncle still loves her," she cried. Her voice shook with anger and pain.

Turning to Sunita, she said, "I will do this alone. I don't want you to lose your friendship with Manan over this."

Unbuckling her seatbelt, Sunita reached over to hug her. "Aren't you my friend too?"

Mira's arms tightened around Sunita as tears threatened again. This girl, whom Mira had once thought to be a rival for Manan's affections, was becoming too dear.

Settling back into the seat, Sunita cleared her throat. Buckling her seatbelt again, she briskly asked, "What do we do next?"

"Let's talk to Dev and find out if he knows anything about Janaki," Mira said, picking up her phone to call Dev.

Half an hour later, both the women were again in front of the black gates. This time, when they pressed the buzzer, the gates immediately swung open. Soon, they were ushered into what seemed to be a family room. There was a sofa near the window with comfortable chairs flanking it. Bay windows looking out into the garden flanked one wall.

It was room for comfort rather than luxury, though, in her current mental state, Mira was oblivious to both. She was trying to ignore the tears that once again tickled the back of her throat as Dev walked towards her.

"Mira! How are you?" he asked, his eyes full of worry for her.

After the altercation with Manan, he had wanted to stay with Mira to console her. But Sunita had quickly bundled Mira into her car and driven off before Dev could catch his bearings. He thought of calling Mira but was unsure if she would be in the frame of mind to take a call. Thus, when Mira called asking about Janaki, he did not hesitate to invite the two women home.

Mira's lips twisted before replying, "I have been better."

Dev pressed her hand in sympathy, wishing he could erase the misery evident in the redness of her eyes. "Anything I can do to help?" he asked.

"As you know, we are searching for a lady called Janaki. This is the last address we found for her in the college records. Do you know anybody in your family with that name?" Mira asked.

Dev shook his head. "No idea, but maybe Grandma can help," he replied, as Mrs. Malhotra walked into the room.

"Help with what?" Mrs. Malhotra asked, before giving a warm hug to Mira.

Drawing back, she looked at Mira's tear-streaked face and asked, "*Beta*, is everything ok?"

The concern in her voice made Mira's lips tremble again. Controlling her emotions, she said, "Yes, Aunty, I am fine."

"Mira and Sunita are looking for a lady called Janaki. As far as I know, there is no Janaki in our family," Dev replied, jumping into the conversation before Mira lost her composure again.

Mrs. Malhotra turned towards Mira and Sunita.

"How do you girls know Janaki?" she asked, her voice sharp.

"You know Janaki?" Sunita asked, bouncing on the balls of her feet.

"I believe I asked first," Mrs. Malhotra replied, her customary cheerful smile missing.

"We don't know Janaki personally, but she is an acquaintance of a gentleman who is dear to us," Mira replied.

"Raghunath..." Mrs. Malhotra whispered.

"Yes!" gasped Mira and Sunita in unison.

Mrs. Malhotra gave a soft cry before she swayed as if her legs couldn't take her weight. Dev lunged forward to support her. "Are you not feeling well, Grandma? Shall I send for the doctor?" he asked, holding her upright as she walked the few steps to the sofa, where she sank into the cushions. She looked frail as if a gust of wind would blow her away.

"Aunty, do you know where and how is Janaki?" Sunita implored, "Uncle still waits for her."

Dev threw Sunita an annoyed look. "Can't you see she is not well? Grandma needs to rest. Maybe you can visit some other day."

Mrs. Malhotra shook her head. Slowly, her spine straightened, and she was once again the Mrs. Malhotra Mira had met at the party, but without the twinkle in her eyes. Patting Dev's cheek, she said, "No, my dear boy. I was just surprised. I am fine now. I will talk to the girls."

Waving a hand towards the chairs, she said, "Why don't you sit down? I will tell you the story while we have tea."

"How much of the story have you heard?" Mrs. Malhotra asked, as a silent-footed servant kept a tea tray on the table in front of her and left the room.

"Till Janaki stopped coming to the coffeehouse," Sunita answered.

"And Raghunath still waits for her?"

"He used to until a few months ago. After his grandson renovated it, changing it into a cafe, he stopped. But we can see the wait in his eyes," replied Mira.

Mrs. Malhotra's eyes softened. "That's why the board was different. I noticed it when we drove through the town."

Looking at the mistiness in Mrs. Malhotra's eyes, Mira felt uneasy. Suspicion bloomed in her heart.

But no, Manan had said, Janaki's full name was Janaki Srivastava.

Pouring a cup of tea, Mrs. Malhotra handed it to Dev as she started narrating the tale.

"Janaki's marriage was fixed with an army officer, Captain Vikram Malhotra. Vikram's family was well-to-do and had barely asked for any dowry. As was the custom in those days, Janaki had not met Vikram before the wedding. She had only seen a photo of him, which showed a handsome, stern-looking man. But, as expected of her, Janaki was prepared to do her duty. However, a month before her wedding, Janaki met Raghunath. She felt an instant connection with him but knew she couldn't break off a good match just because she felt a frisson of awareness for a stranger.

"Janaki could find no fault with Vikram. He was a kind and honourable, but while she respected him, she could not fall in love with him, because unknowingly, she had fallen in love with Raghunath.

"When Raghunath confessed his love for her, she was elated. She had secretly longed to hear those words. But his words also had the potential to bring social shame and stigma to her and her family. Thus, breaking both their hearts, she pushed him away.

"Raghunath however, refused to give up. When Raghunath said he would be at the coffeehouse every day, initially she resisted. But in the end, she succumbed to the temptation. Every day she would tell herself she wouldn't go, and yet, every day at eleven, she would be there. She knew what she was doing was wrong. She was cheating on her husband, if not physically, then emotionally."

The room was silent save for the teacup clattering as Mrs. Malhotra kept it on the table. Her eyes focused on the carpet she remembered the memories she thought she had buried deep in her heart. Sensing her sorrow, Dev wrapped his arms around her. She gave him a wan smile before continuing with her tale.

"Janaki continued to lie to herself and her family for six months. Then Janaki missed her periods. The day the doctor confirmed Janaki was pregnant, she was filled with self-loathing. Two men loved and cherished her. She was playing with emotions of both. Janaki knew it was time to decide. She needed to pick one, either Raghunath or her husband. If she kept visiting the coffeehouse, Raghunath would never give up the hope that one day she would be his. Till the time she kept going to the coffeehouse, she would keep Raghunath in her heart and not give her husband a chance to win her affection. And the little one, taking its first breaths in her womb, would have a mother whose heart belonged to someone she was not bound to.

"But before Janaki could decide, the choice was taken away from her. Her husband was deployed to the front, where tensions were brewing. Vikram was not oblivious. He had sensed Janaki's unhappiness. But unlike Janaki, he was deeply in love with her, though being a man of few words, he had never spoken the words. Knowing the vagaries of war, he decided to confess the emotions of his heart. The night before he was supposed to leave, he took Janaki to the terrace of their house. Lacing his fingers with hers, he looked into her eyes and said, "Janaki, my love, I do not know if I will come back to you or not, but if I don't, remember that I love you with my whole being. You are the reason that I breathe." Placing his hand over her stomach, which was still flat, he said, "I will cherish you and the little one inside until my dying breath."

"Janaki looked into Vikram's eyes full of love and knew what she had to do. She stopped going to the coffeehouse."

The three looked at Mrs. Malhotra in silence, aware that remembering the past was bringing pain

to her.

"What happened after that?" Sunita asked, breaking the silence.

Mrs. Malhotra let out a long sigh. "Vikram's premonition came true. He died a martyr's death on the front, and Janaki became a widow."

"Why didn't she go to Raghunath?" Mira said.

"Do you think Raghunath's family would have accepted a pregnant widow as their daughter-in-law?" Mrs. Malhotra asked scornfully. "We are talking about a time when the rules of society were rigid. Moreover, Janaki knew she couldn't dishonour Vikram's love and let another raise his child. She decided to leave the town and settle in a new place. A place where there were no memories to haunt her.

"But she couldn't erase the past completely. Her family was still here. She stayed in touch but refused to come back. The family thought she was doing it because she loved Vikram so much that remaining in the same town caused her pain. But the truth was, she didn't want any chance of meeting Raghunath. She knew if she met Raghunath, she would weaken. She did not want to betray Vikram and his love."

"Was Janaki happy with her decision?" Mira asked.

Mrs. Malhotra gave her a sad smile. "She was content. And contentment is harder to find than happiness."

"Where is Janaki now?" Mira asked, her voice soft.

Mrs. Malhotra gave her a steady look. Standing up, she said, "It has been a long day. I think I will call it a night."

Dev started getting up to help her, but she waved him off, "I am ok, I can go to my room." Adjusting her saree pallu, she walked towards the door, her bearing regal. At the door, she turned back to look at Dev. "I think tomorrow I would like to have coffee at this cafe," she said, before leaving the room.

The three sat shell-shocked for a few moments before Mira turned toward Sunita. "Are you thinking what I am thinking?"

Sunita grinned back at her.

Dev shook his head, "No, this can't be happening!"

Two sets of eyes turned towards him. Looking at their expression, he sputtered, "You guys honestly believe Grandma is the Janaki you were searching for?"

They both nodded.

"But how...?" he muttered, slumping into the sofa and clutching his hair.

"This is the last known address of Janaki's from the college records. The story your grandmother told us explains why Janaki stopped coming. Only Janaki or someone very close to her would have known the story," Sunita pointed out.

"Grandma is Janaki...I can't believe it," Dev said. His actions were jerky as he stood up to pace the room.

"This town is where I have always seen her at peace, and yet, I never asked her why she made excuses not to visit. I always assumed it was because of the issues with the rest of my grandfather's family who resented her since he left everything to her in his will. This time, she came because I insisted, I needed her to resolve a legal tangle," he continued.

"Are you ok, Dev?" Mira asked, concerned as Dev's words tumbled out faster.

Dev looked at her. The breath escaped his lips in a soft sigh. Shrugging, he said, "I am not sure. Knowing that Grandma is Janaki, and she loved someone who was not my grandfather, is not something one can process in a few minutes. I am not oblivious. I saw how she looked when she talked about Raghunath. There was this softness around her I have never seen before. Remember I told you? She had a hard life?"

Mira nodded.

"I just want her to be happy," he continued. "Even if the truth is sitting weirdly in my stomach, making me want to throw up!"

"Yes, yes, all that is fine. You will work out your feelings etc. Let's move on to why we are here," Sunita said, jumping into the conversation. Ignoring the reproachful look Mira threw at her, she shrugged. "Well, one of us needs to be practical. Feelings can be sorted out later. Mira, you need to get Raghu Uncle to the cafe tomorrow."

Mira shook her head, "You saw how angry Manan was. He will not let me talk to Raghu Uncle. I think either of you should go."

Crouching in front of Mira, Sunita took Mira's hands in hers.

"Mira, this search for Janaki was your idea. You were the one who realized that Uncle needed closure. Now that we have found her, it is only fitting that you be the one who tells him about her."

"You must!" insisted Dev, coming to stand in front of Mira. "You have come so far, don't let anything stop you now."

Looking at their faces, full of expectations, Mira realised the truth. She didn't want to, but she would have to face Manan again. For Janaki and Raghunath.

XXII

At nine the next morning, Mira stood at the door of Manan's house, willing her finger to press the doorbell. She had spent the night at Sunita's home, unwilling to face Manan when her emotions were still raw. Seeing her tense face as she got ready in the morning, Sunita offered to come with her for moral support.

Mira, however, rejected the offer. She had toyed with visiting Raghunath after Manan had left for the cafe but decided against it. She didn't want to take the coward's way out and hide things from Manan anymore. Sooner or later, she would have to face Manan. Moreover, it was time to confess everything to Raghunath.

The decision to go to the cafe would be his alone. Not Manan's. Not Mira's.

A sudden gust of breeze made the crepe myrtle tree at the gate sway. Mira suppressed a shiver. She didn't know whether it was because of the chill of the breeze or because she was about to face Manan.

Taking a deep breath, she pressed the doorbell. Mira heard footsteps before the door opened to reveal Manan. Tiredness showed in his eyes, and his usually neat hair was standing up in all directions. Even his shirt was half-hanging out. Mira felt her heart give a loud thump. She wanted to run a hand to smooth down his hair but controlled herself.

Without crossing the doorway, she stated, "I want to meet Uncle."

Manan looked at her, his face impassive, before inclining his head.

She followed him into the kitchen, where Raghunath sat cradling a cup of tea.

"Good morning, *beta ji*! Did you have a good time with Sunita?" he asked cheerfully. "Manan told me you are planning to stay with her for a few days."

Mira looked at Manan reproachfully. "You didn't tell him?"

Manan flushed at the accusation in her tone.

Puzzled, Raghunath questioned, "Tell me what?"

The two stayed quiet, staring at each other from across the room, their backs stiff and unyielding. Realising something was amiss, he asked, "Did you both argue?"

"I didn't fight. Manan fought with me," Mira said plaintively, knowing she sounded childishly petulant.

"If you had not hidden things from me, I would not have fought," Manan retorted.

"I hid things because I knew you were going to be unreasonable. And I was proven right," Mira shot back.

"I am not unreasonable in protecting the person I love!" He roared, banging his plate on the kitchen counter.

"Children, please!" Raghunath jumped into the argument, "Will someone please tell me what's going on?" Patting the chair next to him, he said to Mira, "Come *beta ji*, you tell me everything."

Mira dashed away angry tears that had spilled over her cheeks as she did his bidding.

Cradling his gnarled hands in hers, she looked into his kind eyes. Deciding not to beat around the bush, she said, "Sunita and I tried to search for Janaki."

Raghunath started, his face turning pale.

Instantly Manan was by his side, "*Dadu*! Are you ok?" Turning to Mira, he shouted, "Look what you have done!"

Before Mira could reply, Raghunath held up his hand to stop Manan.

"Did you find her?" he asked, his hands clutching Mira's as if she were his lifeline. His voice was full of love and longing.

Mira answered, "We should be at the cafe at eleven."

"Can't you see *Dadu* is not well? He is not going anywhere," Manan objected.

Ignoring Manan, Mira looked steadily at Raghunath. He held her gaze for a few moments before giving her a nod.

"No, *Dadu*, you can't go," Manan implored.

Raghunath patted Manan's arm gently. "One last time, my boy. One last time."

****

The bell on the cafe's door tinkled as the woman entered. The cafe was empty except for an elderly gentleman seated at the table in the back, an open book in front of him.

Their eyes met, and a shy smile bloomed on her face. Years had passed, yet today, her heart was galloping like a giddy nineteen-year-old meeting her lover for a first date.

Afraid that excitement might make her trip, she walked deliberately slowly, as her eyes took in the changes the years had wrought in him. He was still in a tweed jacket, though it now hung over his frame, and there was a slight stoop in his shoulders. His mop of dark curls was now a few wispy tufts of white. This was a man who had seen many seasons and challenges. But despite all the changes, he still looked like the Raghunath who had captured her heart many moons ago.

She could feel his eyes on her as well. *What does he see?* She wondered for the years had changed her too. Her face was no longer smooth and unlined but a mass of wrinkles. Her pride and joy, the hair that had once cascaded down her back as a black waterfall, was now a silver bob, skimming her chin.

She drew the *pallu* of her beige silk saree around her shoulders, clutching it tighter, as she reached closer.

He stood up as she approached the table.

"You look the same," she blurted.

He grinned at her before saying, "Ditto."

They laughed at the blatant lie before sitting down. Silence descended on the table as they looked at each other, content to drink in their fill of each other.

"I am sorry, Raghu," she said, breaking the silence.

Placing a hand over hers, he replied, "Don't be."

"But you were stuck in a time loop waiting for me. I did not have the courage to face you."

"You did not ask me to wait, Janaki. It was my decision," Raghunath replied.

"But would you still have waited if I had not come even once?"

When Mira told her that Raghunath had waited for her all these years, the guilt in her heart for betraying

Raghunath compounded. She couldn't get rid of the suspicion that she had given him false hope when she had come to the coffeehouse for those six months.

"I still would have waited," he replied.

His voice was low, but she could hear his honesty, his love, in the words. She looked back at him, silent, her eyes bright with unshed tears.

"I love you," Raghunath said.

"Oh, Raghu! I love you too! But I never dared to take what I wanted. And once I was free from responsibilities, I assumed you would have moved on. I didn't have faith in your love," Janaki replied, the pain in her heart making her voice quiver.

Raghunath shrugged. "It is all in the past. You are here now, and that is all that matters. One day, we will revisit the past. You will tell me the challenges you faced, for your face tells me of the battles you have fought. But today, all I want to do is savour the sight of you and inhale your perfume."

Janaki smiled at Raghu's last statement.

The years fell away. They were once more Janaki and Raghu who had fallen in love for the first time.

From near the kitchen door, Dev, Sunita, Manan and Mira stood silently, watching Janaki and Raghunath engrossed in each other.

"After you guys left, I asked Grandma why I didn't know that her name was Janaki. She said that my grandfather's family changed her name to Gayatri at the time of the wedding," Dev whispered.

"No wonder we didn't put two and two together when we first met Mrs. Malhotra. Imagine if we had known her name was Janaki, we would have asked her outright, right in the beginning," chuckled Sunita.

At that moment, Raghunath placed his hands on Janaki's and whispered something that made her blush.

Dev shook his head. "It feels funny to see your grandmother blush."

Sunita gave him a mischievous look. "I presume you know enough biology to know what will happen if they decide to get married."

"Married? Why would they want to get married?" Dev asked, horrified.

"Because these two people, who loved each other and were forced apart by circumstances, are finally together. Since they do not belong to a generation that considers live-in as a proof of relationship, I do not think they will want to waste even a minute now."

Dev clutched his head, groaning. "You are an evil person to be putting such ideas in my mind!" He said to Sunita.

"That I am," replied Sunita, giving him a cheeky grin.

As Sunita and Dev squabbled, Manan and Mira kept quiet.

Mira could feel Manan's forbidding presence by her side. Her senses tingled with his proximity, yet she couldn't forget the harsh words spoken by him. Looking at Janaki and Raghunath laughing and talking, she felt her heart throb with pain. She had succeeded in bringing two lovers together but had lost Manan.

"I am going back tomorrow," she announced.

Dev and Sunita stopped arguing to stare at her.

"But you still have a few days of your holidays left," Sunita objected.

"Nothing is keeping me here any longer," Mira replied.

"But...," Dev started to argue.

Ignoring him, Mira walked towards Raghunath as he beckoned her.

She could feel Manan's eyes boring into her back, but she refused to glance at him.

XXIII

The zip whirred as Mira closed her suitcase before flopping down on her back on the bed. That's it. Her packing was done, the taxi was booked for early morning to drive her back to town, and there was nothing more to be done except turn in for the night.

Unblinking, she stared at the ceiling. Mira knew that sleep would not come tonight. Earlier in the cafe, her decision to leave had surprised Raghunath and Janaki. They tried cajoling and emotionally blackmailing her, but Mira did not budge from her decision. She knew she couldn't.

To stay in the town would mean constantly meeting Manan. Their lives were too intertwined here. But if she left, the distance would dull the pain.

Probably.

A knock at the door broke the thoughts that threatened to draw her into the darkness. She opened the door to see

Raghunath standing there, a glass of milk in his hand.

"You skipped dinner, saying you had to pack, so I brought you some milk. You shouldn't sleep with an empty stomach."

Mira felt guilt stab in her heart, seeing the concern in his eyes. She knew her abrupt decision to leave had hurt him. "I wish I didn't have to leave, but I cannot stay here any longer," she replied, hoping Raghunath would understand her hasty decision.

Raghunath gently patted her back. "I know, my dear. Loving someone is painful."

Mira looked at him in surprise. Raghunath gave a low chuckle. "I am old my dear, but not blind. I know you are in love with Manan. It is quite evident in the way your eyes always search for him."

Giving her a final pat, he said, "Drink the milk and go to sleep. A new day always brings a fresh perspective."

Wearily, Mira nodded as Raghunath shuffled down the corridor into his room. Placing the glass of milk on the bedside table, she went back to close her door when she saw Manan standing a few feet away, staring at her. Unwilling to get into a battle of wills with him, Mira gently closed her bedroom door.

Within five minutes, there was another knock on the door.

Mira knew it was him. She wanted to pretend she had already gone to sleep, but knew it was a childish ploy to delay the inevitable. If Raghunath and Janaki's story had taught her something, it was, to be honest in a relationship. The sooner they ended things and said whatever needed to be said, the easier it would be for her to move on.

Moreover, it was he who had been wrong. After the tenderness of the picnic, his anger had been difficult to swallow. He had shouted at her in front of everybody at the cafe, refusing to listen to her point of view, humiliating her in front of friends and strangers. Thinking about the incident in the cafe sparked Mira's anger. Stomping to the door, she wrenched it open.

"What?" she snarled.

"You look terrible," Manan said, taking in her eyes that were red with all the crying she had done in the past two days.

"Have you come here to insult me?" she retorted.

His reply was a shrug as he brushed past her to walk into the room with a swagger.

"I didn't invite you to enter my room," she said, resisting the childish urge to shove him out.

"The house is mine, ergo the room also belongs to me," he replied, removing her suitcase to sprawl on the bed.

"Fine. I will call Sunita or Dev and ask them to take me to their house. I refuse to stay where I have no privacy," Mira said, trying to ignore how at ease he looked on the bed she slept in every night.

She moved to the table to pick up her phone. Instantly, Manan reached out and plucked the phone from her hand. Mira was stunned by his actions.

"Give me back my phone!" she demanded through clenched teeth.

"No."

"I will call Uncle and tell him you are a bully," she warned.

"*Dadu* has gone to sleep and is, no doubt, dreaming about his Janaki. And I know you wouldn't want to come between *Dadu* and Janaki, now that they are finally together," he taunted.

Mira took a deep breath, trying to ignore the alluring scent of cologne that teased. With exaggerated calm, she said, "Manan, I am asking you again. Give me my phone!"

Manan shook his head. "Not until you talk to me."

Mira whirled away to stand at the window. She stared into the darkness beyond, her knuckles turning white as she clutched the windowsill. "There is nothing left to talk about."

"We need to talk about you leaving the town, even though you still have a few days of your holidays left."

"There is nothing left for me here," she said, still looking out of the window.

Coming to stand behind her, Manan wrapped his arms around her, drawing her body against his. "So, you would deny what is between us?" he growled next to her ear, his breath fanning across her cheeks.

Looking at their reflection in the windowpane, his arms around her, Mira could feel an answering tingle in her heart. She wanted to sag her body against his, revel in his warmth, but she resisted.

Keeping her spine straight, she said, "I do not deny the physical attraction between us, but that is all there is to our relationship. If we can call it that."

Manan turned her around to face him. "How can you say that, Mira?" he demanded. Placing her hand over his heart, he said, "Can't you feel how heavy my heart is at the thought of you going away? It is more than physical attraction, and you know it, Mira. You feel it in the bones, the way I do."

Mira wrenched her hand away. Her lips trembled as she said, "You made your feelings very clear, Manan when you asked me to leave the cafe. You pointed out that I have no right to interfere in your life."

Manan pulled her closer. His voice was gentle as he said, "I am sorry, Mira, I truly am. I was in a state of shock. The day before, I had shared my life story with you. I thought we shared a connection, a bond. I couldn't believe that you were keeping secrets from me, and that too about Janaki. A woman I disliked."

"So, you took out your dislike for her on me?" Mira cried. The tears were now falling unchecked.

Manan wiped them away with a gentle finger. "Don't cry, my love. I was wrong, and I am sorry for that. In my heart, I knew that your actions were because you cared deeply for *Dadu* and wanted him to be happy. I was just scared that *Dadu* would be hurt again. My fear made me lash at you in anger. Please, please forgive me?" he pleaded.

Mira moved away from his arms. "I am and always will be someone who believes in the power of love. And you will always be someone who doesn't believe in it. You didn't trust me enough not to hurt you. We are incompatible, Manan."

"Are you breaking up with me?" he demanded, his voice harsh.

"We were never together for this to be a break-up, Manan. No words were spoken. No promises were made," she replied.

Manan's eyes glittered as he stared at her. And then, in two steps, he had her again in his arms. Cradling her face in his palms, he raised her face, forcing her to look into his eyes.

"You want the words? I will give you words. You are like a thorn in my heart, making me ache constantly. I think of you when you are not with me, and when you are, all I can think of is kissing you.

"Yes, I did not believe in the power of love, but that was only until I met you. I love you! I love your laugh, the way you get so engrossed in your book that you become oblivious to your surroundings, your love for *Dadu*, and your infernal tenacity in not giving up on Janaki.

"I love you, Mira Rajput! And if you leave me tomorrow, I will follow you to the ends of the earth and hound you until you say that you love me too!"

Mira stared into Manan's eyes, seeing the love and honesty shining in them as he said the words she longed to hear. Her eyelids fluttered shut as his lip descended on hers, taking possession of her heart and senses.

Many minutes later, when they surfaced for air, Manan nipped her lips gently, whispering, "Say it, Mira."

Mira opened her eyes, her eyes dazed.

"Say what?" she asked, puzzled.

"Say that you love me," he demanded.

"I love you, Manan, today and always," Mira whispered.

XXIV

Let us go then, you and I,
When the evening is spread out against the sky.

"Where are you?" a gruff voice asked.

"I have just reached Cafe Sunshine, Daddy," Sunita replied.

"You need to be home by eight for the dinner with the American delegation," he replied.

"But I already have plans with my friends here," Sunita replied.

"I still hold your purse strings," came the brusque warning that had Sunita clutching the steering wheel until her knuckles turned white.

Before Sunita could reply, another voice came over the phone. Sweet and cloying the words made Sunita's stomach churn. "Sunita darling, please do listen to what your dad is saying. Mr. Mehra's son, Varun, will also be there. We have such high hopes for both of you. Do come *na*, it will be fun."

As always, when Sunita's mother spoke to her in these tones, Sunita knew it was futile to argue.

"I will think about it," was her only answer.

"And darling, stop mingling with these middle-class people. Please remember you are the future of Kailash Industries," her mother cooed before disconnecting the call.

Sunita sat with her shoulders slumped, seeing the sign of Cafe Sunshine swing in the evening breeze. Phone calls with her parents left her feeling trapped, buried under the weight of being the only daughter of Kailash Sharma.

Her mother's words about being the future of Kailash Industries were a half-truth. Sunita would never be allowed to run Kailash Industries. She was nothing but a commodity to be bartered as a bride to someone handpicked by her parents, who would finally run Kailash Industries. Her education and qualifications were worthless for her parents who, in the past year, had dropped big enough hints that it was time that the business deal of her marriage took place. That Varun Mehra would also be at the dinner meant back-door dealings of her future marriage had already started.

Sunita swallowed, trying to avoid the tears that threatened to fall. Her father might be the richest man in town, but she was powerless. She couldn't escape the future her parents were planning for her.

A knock on the car window startled her. It was Dev, giving her a cheeky grin. Sunita smiled back, rolling down the window.

"We saw you park more than fifteen minutes ago! Everyone is waiting for you! Are you planning to stay in the car the whole evening or are you coming into the cafe?" he asked.

Poking his head inside, he said, "Your car is nice, but too small to spend the night in!" he teased.

Sunita chuckled while getting out of the car. As they walked together towards the cafe, she replied, "At least it is better than someone else's car, which got stuck in the market the day before!"

Dev gave an embarrassed laugh at the memory of his Jeep Compass being stuck for two hours in the market, creating a humongous traffic jam.

Sunita, however, wasn't done with him yet. "You do know what they say when some men like a big car," she said.

Opening the cafe door, Dev asked, "What?"

Leaning towards him, she whispered in an exaggerated stage whisper, "That those people are compensating for a lack of size somewhere else!"

Laughing at his annoyed gasp, she walked in leaving Dev behind.

Manan had closed the cafe early at Sunita's urging. She said they needed to celebrate the happily ever after of the two couples. Manan had retorted that if he kept closing the cafe early to celebrate stuff, soon there would be no cafe left. But the twinkle in his eyes had tendered his words useless.

Predictably, Raghu Uncle was seated at his favourite corner table. But instead of reading or looking up whenever the cafe door opened, he was clapping to the beats of the music as Manan and Mira showed off their dance moves.

Sunita grinned as Manan twirled Mira into a spin before bending her backwards on his arm and kissing her thoroughly.

"You two need to get a room," she called out.

"You, my dear," Manan replied, hugging a giggling Mira closer, "Are jealous that we have found love!"

"Yeah right," she scoffed, still not able to believe how different Manan looked after confessing his love to Mira. He looked softer now that he finally believed in the power of love.

At least one of us did, she thought, taking a chair next to Dev.

"Something smells different," she said, scrunching up her nose.

"It may be the cinnamon from my carrot cake," said Janaki, coming out from the kitchen door, a perfectly frosted carrot cake in her hand. Raghunath beamed at Janaki with quiet pride as Manan whistled appreciatively.

"Ooh! Yes!" Mira said, reaching forward to take the cake from Janaki, "I have had a taste of Aunty's cake and can vouch for it to be the best!"

Dev scowled. Looking suspiciously at the cake, he demanded, "What do you want, Grandma? What is on your mind?"

Janaki blushed at the accusation in his tone before replying, "Well, as you all know, Raghu and I have loved each other for many years."

The others chuckled at her understatement.

"Well, you see…" she started again, wringing her hands.

Placing his hands on hers, Raghunath said, "Let's talk plainly, my dear. Children, Janaki and I have decided to get married. We have set the date a month from today."

Manan and Mira jumped up to congratulate Janaki and Raghunath. Sunita whispered, "I told you so," to Dev before getting up to hug Janaki.

"But Grandma," Dev's serious voice cut through their joy. "What about the legal dispute of the house?"

"What legal dispute?" Manan asked, handing out plates to everyone.

"The dispute, my dears, is my husband's younger brother trying to stake a claim on our house here. He thinks that since Captain Malhotra passed away before my son, Ajay, was born, he has the right to the ancestral house here. All these years, out of a sense of family duty or maybe because of the guilt that I never loved Vikram the way he deserved, I have been paying him money whenever he threatened to take the matter to court. But after Dev's product launch, when he sent another demanding letter, I decided to fight back. That house belonged to Captain Malhotra and is now Dev's. I refuse to give it up to anyone. This was the reason why we came back to town. To prove ownership. Dev thought staying for a few weeks in the house would strengthen our case," Janaki explained.

"And I am very glad you decided to fight, my love. Otherwise, I would still be waiting for you," replied Raghunath, kissing her knuckles.

Janaki squeezed his hand affectionately before turning back to Dev. "You are confident we will win the case?"

Dev nodded.

"Then I see no reason to postpone my happiness," she replied.

"But what about the cafe in the city? Will you walk away from years of hard work, just to get married?" Dev's voice was harsh as he demanded the answer.

Sunita gave an exasperated sigh. "What are you doing, Dev? Finally, they are together and happy. Why are you creating problems when there aren't any?"

Janaki shook her head to stop Sunita from saying anything more. Leaving Raghunath's side, she walked to Dev. Patting his cheek gently, she said, "I know you love me a lot, Dev. For so many years, it has been just the two of us against the world. I know you are worried about me, but I have lost too many years bowing to societal norms. I now want to enjoy the time I have left with Raghunath and do what my heart desires. Even if you are not happy with my decision, we will still get married." Her voice was soft, but Dev could hear the steel in them.

"And as far as the cafe is concerned, I had a plan, but now it needs to change," she added.

"What plan, Aunty?" Mira asked.

"Well, first I wondered if you would be interested in taking over the cafe. But since you have already decided to move here, and I need someone who could supervise the cafe personally, I will now hire someone else."

"So, you will hand over the cafe to a stranger?" Dev asked.

Janaki shrugged. "Not the best scenario, but it will have to do. At my age, carpe diem becomes a little too literal. Now how about I serve cake to everyone?"

Dev opened his mouth once again to protest, but this time, Sunita beat him to it.

"I can do it!" the words jumped out of her mouth before she could think

Janaki lifted a brow enquiringly at her.

"I mean, I can help with the café, not the cake," she blurted before continuing. "I helped Manan with renovations and learned so much about running a cafe at that time. Do you think...is it possible that instead of you hiring someone, I take over the running of your cafe?" Sunita's words tapered off. She could feel her ears getting warmer as the others stared at her.

"Are you sure? It is not going to be easy. It is a cafe in a city, with a different sort of clientele," Janaki warned.

Sunita thought back to the conversation she had just had with her parents and the inkling that they might be fixing her match with Varun. This was her one chance to escape their machinations. She was tired of them making decisions for her.

Forcing her spine straight, she smiled. With all the conviction in her heart, she said, "Yes!"

Janki smiled back. "It is settled then. You will handle my cafe in the city." Forking a bite of carrot cake in Sunita's mouth, she said, "To new beginnings."

"To new beginnings," the others echoed.

"To new beginnings," Sunita whispered.

Acknowledgement

A writer doesn't exist in a vacuum. There is an entire ecosystem of people who help a person become a writer.

The most important, of course, is you, dear reader. I would not be a writer if you had not picked up this book. So, thank you!

This book would not have been possible without the contributions of my beta readers: Vipasha, Pratibha, Varunika, Sudha, and Tanvi. Your support was invaluable. I also owe my gratitude to team Purrple Lens for their detailed feedback. It really helped me in working out the kinks in the book.

I am grateful to Kush, Rishabh, and the rest of the family who supported me unflinchingly.

And always, a special thanks to Ashish. I would not have reached here if you had not supported me in this journey. Thank you for being my sounding board and helping me with everything technical.

Over A Cup Of Espresso

Every day at eleven in the morning, she would walk in. He would already be there, waiting.

Every day their eyes would meet over the rims of their cups of espressos. Some days, their gazes would hold, communicating wordlessly. On other days, they would look away as if embarrassed by the ardency of their desire. Both knew their story could proceed no further. By the laws of society, they were bound, to someone else. Yet, some invisible force would bring them to the cafe every day.

Until, one day, she stopped coming.

He still goes to the cafe every day, waiting.

ॐ

This is the hundred-word story that was the seed for Love Awaits, A Tale of Unbroken Promises. The story is now a part of my book, Potpourri Of Drabble.

LIST OF QUOTES USED IN THE BOOK

About the Author

Harshita Nanda is an author, blogger and book reviewer based in Dubai, UAE. She trained as an engineer before changing tracks to become a full-time writer. Her stories have a strong emotional quotient with a streak of feminism. Avoiding unnecessary drama, she focuses on the universal appeal of human emotions.

She published her first book, **Xanadu: Three Souls Searching For Paradise**, in 2021, followed by **BITS and Pieces: A Collage of My BITSian Memories**, in 2022 and **Potpourri of Drabble: A Collection of 100 micro-tales** in 2023.

She was one of the shortlisted candidates for the Rama Mehta Writing Grant, 2023 and her short stories have found a home in many anthologies such as The Blogchatter Book Of Thrillers, The Blogchatter Book of Love, and Lightning Strikes, An Anthology of Flash Fiction by Indian Writers. Her words have appeared on websites like Kitaab, Porch Lit Mag and Roi Faineant Literary Press.

She can be reached on X at @ashnhash and on Instagram at @author_harshita.

OTHER BOOKS BY THE AUTHOR

Xanadu: Three Souls Searching For Their Paradise
BITS and Pieces: A Collage Of My BITSian Memories
Potpourri Of Drabble: A Collection of 100 Micro Tales

Anthologies

The Blogchatter Book of Love
The Blogchatter Book of Thrillers
Lightning Strikes
Letters To Santa
Disobedient Girls
Strings Of Humanity
ALS 2022 : An Anthology of Short Stories and Articles
Airavata
Life During Covid-19
Navigating Covid-19